They Said It Was Murder

THEY SAID IT WAS MURDER

Elizabeth Sheppard

The Book Guild Ltd.
Sussex, England

This book is a work of fiction. The characters and situations in this story are imaginary. No resemblance is intended between these characters and any real persons, either living or dead.

The Book Guild Ltd.
25 High Street,
Lewes, Sussex.

First published 1992

Set in Baskerville
Typesetting by Ashford Setting & Design,
Ashford, Middlesex.
Printed in Great Britain by
Antony Rowe Ltd.,
Chippenham, Wiltshire.

A catalogue record for this book is
available from the British Library

ISBN 0 86332 803 2

1

'You want to marry that yokel, that clodhopper, you must be out of your mind.'

'You don't understand Father, I don't want to marry him, I've got to,' replied Janet.

'Got to! If you mean what I think you mean you ought to be ashamed of yourself, it's a good thing your poor mother isn't alive to see this day, it would have broken her heart. He had better keep away from me, he deserves a good horsewhipping.'

Charles Collet's mind was working furiously. His thoughts were a mixture of anger, shame and mental wondering, wondering what to do next. His wife had died suddenly, killed outside his own front door. His only daughter was now fifteen years old, he loved her so much. He had thought to solace himself after his wife's sudden death by marrying almost at once a childhood sweetheart. Ada had been close at hand and he had mistakenly thought that Janet would welcome a new mother. The new mother, however, had lost no time in persuading her father to send her away to a boarding school. Janet and her father had previously been inseparable but Janet's hatred of her new mother seemed to know no bounds.

'You don't have to marry that scoundrel you know,' said Father when he had digested the news and cooled down a bit, 'I expect I could arrange with one of your aunts to have you for a while and look after you, we could fix something up.'

'No, I would rather get married, you are wrong about Sam, he is a good son to his mother. We might be able to live in a cottage in a farm. There is a farmer, the one that Sam works for, he has offered Sam the cottage as soon as it is ready. All we need is the money to buy some furniture and things, I would much rather live there anyway than anywhere else and I have hated staying at school. We can keep some little chickens if we like and a lovely big sheep dog. We shall be all right and Sam's mother is a nice woman. She lives in the village quite near the farm.'

'Where is this farm?' asked Charles Collet.

'It's right away from the road and in the country near Warwick.'

'How on earth did you come to get mixed up with his fellow?'

'I met him when I went to stay at Mary Burn's farm that time. He used to see us when we walked the greyhounds. I told you Mary's sister was a trainer didn't I? We all went coursing in the Cotswolds together you know, after wild hares.'

Janet was quite excited, remembering the wonderful time she had spent with her friend that day. 'Sam was in charge of the dogs, they called him the Slipper because he had to let the dogs loose when the hare appeared, he is really quite nice you know.'

'Oh well,' said Father, 'I will make you an allowance since you seem to have made up your mind and give you a sum of money for your furniture. That will be the end. Don't expect me to come to the wedding. I will have washed my hands of you completely, your new mother must not be told about this.'

* * *

After this episode Janet and Sam were soon married and went to stay with Sam's mother until their cottage was ready. She was a bad-tempered old lady and lost no opportunity to tell Janet what a favour she was doing in letting her stay there, and when the baby arrived she insisted that it should spend most of its time in an old pram they had acquired, outside in the small garden. Janet spent much time trying to keep the child out of the way, helping in the house and trying to avoid the daily visits of Maud, her husband's sister who lived a few doors away and was intensely jealous of Janet. She continually reminded her, in what she thought was a high-class imitative accent, that she was 'putting on' the old lady. Janet could scarcely wait for the cottage to be ready. The child seemed to realize that he must not make a noise and slept peacefully for hours in the garden. Sometimes Janet would forget that he was there, then suddenly she would remember that he had to be fed. She would hastily heat milk and take out his bottle, waiting nearby until the bottle was empty or the child was asleep again. Maud would often appear, she seemed to have few of the ordinary small household utensils and frequently came to borrow the flat iron, which she heated in front of the kitchen fire, or perhaps a baking tin, some salt or sugar, scissors or cotton or sometimes bread. She would glance at the baby lying in the pram, roughly pull aside his covers and sniff loudly. Mother would often say, 'That child is crying again', and Janet would drop her work and rush out to see, only to find that young Charles was fast asleep as usual. Janet was now able to earn a little money sewing for neighbours at her mother-in-law's instigation.

'If you hadn't been silly enough to get yourself pregnant you could have got a job sewing in one of the big houses and made our Sam a good wife, you are quite handy with a needle I must say.'

Maud also remarked that it was a pity that the young couple had to burden themselves with a child so soon. 'You are taking a risk you know, leaving him out in the garden alone like you do. There's Billy the gipsy, you know, the one who comes round with his wife to grind scissors, they often come round this way. Look well if you find the pram empty one of these days.'

'Oh,' replied Mother, 'no one else would want to be burdened with that child but they might feel envious and push the covers over his face.'

'What a silly idea,' said Janet.

All the same, she looked out a little more often after those remarks. One day Mother had set her a more time-consuming job than usual. It was wash-day and this was always a hard and long chore. Suddenly Janet thought of Charles. 'Goodness, he hasn't had his midday bottle.' She hurriedly prepared it and took it outside to the pram. Charles did not look his usual placid self, he was lying on his stomach, his face buried in the pillow and fear shot through Janet's heart as she turned him over. He seemed to be fast asleep. 'Or dead', thought Janet in a panic. She rushed into the house and upstairs to Mother. 'Come and look at Charles quickly,' she shouted, dragging Mrs Smith down the stairs. 'You went into the garden just now to look at the clothes, did you look at the baby?'

'No I didn't,' replied Mrs Smith, 'I don't dote on the child like you do, Maud was here, ask her.' Mrs Smith walked out to the pram and picked up the child. 'You had better send for the doctor,' she said. 'He doesn't seem to be breathing.'

The child was dead. An inquest was held. The report read: Death from something unknown. It was one of those mysterious 'cot deaths' and there was much whispering throughout the village. The local paper sent a reporter to ask for details but Sam's mother proved a good ally and soon turned him away. Gossip gradually died down and much relief was felt when Same cam home with the news that the cottage was ready. When Janet stood waiting her turn in the crowded village shop mothers would snatch their children away. She vowed that she would go into the town to do her shopping when they were installed in their new home. Maud lost no opportunity in saying how sorry she was that her brother had picked a murderess for a wife. Sam grew very annoyed at his sister's remarks but hesitated to reprimand her. He was a stolid, peace-loving man and only wished to be left alone with his work that he enjoyed, and his wife who he thought was far above him and him family in status and education. A letter was composed and sent to Janet's father asking for the promised cash for their furniture. Charles Collet put a cheque in an envelope, addressed it and added on a scrap of paper, 'Don't ask for any more.'

2

'Can I give you a lift?' The new looking car stopped and the smiling driver opened the door invitingly. 'I am going into Warwick.'

Janet looked at the smiling face and decided to accept the offer. It was another two miles into town and already she had walked almost a mile. It was a warm day and she felt quite relieved and a little excited. Life was very dull and at times the lack of any luxury and the hard and lonely life became disheartening. A conversation started and the girl found herself confiding in the polite stranger, he was a pleasant middle-aged man who reminded her somewhat of her father. 'Yes, I live on a farm. It is nice place really. We are a long way from the road, two fields actually but we have a nice orchard, with lots of fruit, lovely fresh eggs and milk and butter, I am going into town to get some small things and order what groceries we need. They are usually delivered but there is sure to be something that we have forgotten.'

'Surely you are not going to carry the things home yourself?' asked the stranger.

'Oh, I am used to it and usually I like the walk,' replied Janet.

'I only have one call to make at Warwick,' said the stranger, 'if you like I can meet you somewhere and give you a lift back.' Janet thought for a minute then she accepted the offer. She went about her shopping with a mounting feeling of excitement. Very little adventure came her way, she loved her husband, at least she thought she did, he was kind to her in his way but always was so tired. The day's work on the farm started at six am. First the sheep had to be visited in an outlying field and any attention that was necessary could take a long time. Breakfast was sometimes quite dried up. Sam was always in a hurry but a good breakfast was very necessary as midday dinner was also a moveable feast.

True to his word the obliging stranger was waiting with his car and Janet quite thankfully climbed in. A conversation started again and Janet found herself pouring out her resentment at the fairness of life in general. It soon became obvious to her that the stranger thought she was the daughter of a local landowner, she was quite well dressed in country fashion. Her good quality tweeds were a hand down from the boss's daughter who was away at school most of the time. Janet decided to keep up the idea, surely she could live up to it for a short time, it was rather exciting really.

'We do have bread and fuel delivered of course and we keep ponies to ride.'

'I suppose you ride to hounds?'

'Yes of course.'

Soon the end of the road was reached and it was time to part. 'Do you walk this way often?' asked the stranger.

'Yes, quite often,' replied Janet.

'I will look out for you when I come this way again, it will be in two weeks' time, about the same time of day.'

'Perhaps I will see you then,' replied Janet, and said goodbye as she walked away.

Janet was conscious of a mounting feeling of excitement as the time drew near for her next encounter with the polite stranger. She dressed very carefully and prayed for a fine day. At last the day came. It was bright and sunny as she set off for the town. When she reached the main road she could not resist looking round expectantly at each car that overtook her. She was almost at the end of her journey when the stranger drew up at her side. She greeted him with pleasure and eagerly climbed into the car. 'Get your shopping done and we will take a ride through the wood,' said her friend. 'I see that there is a much-used track a short way back.'

Janet felt rather apprehensive at this remark but when he added, 'I have tea with me and we can have a picnic' she felt very happy at the idea. She hurried through her calls and was waiting as arranged.

'You are a very attractive girl, please call me Donald. I am married, I will be truthful with you, this is a snap of my daughter.'

Janet took the snap and saw a serious-faced girl sitting on a tired looking pony. 'What about your wife?' she asked.

'She no longer has any time for me,' was the reply, and Donald ventured a kiss.

The two enjoyed a cup of thermos tea and a sandwich together. Greatly daring, Donald remarked that he was a commercial traveller and had a journey to take in two weeks' time to see his firm's manager and make his report. It would be at head office in Liverpool. 'How would you like to come with me?' he suggested. 'I would take care of you and bring you back safely, we could go to a show in the evening and we would have to stay overnight.'

Janet was very tempted to take advantage of this exciting offer but could not think how she could manage to stay away overnight. Donald could see that she was tempted by the offer and added, 'I am already very fond of you my dear, I have a daughter of my own and I will see that no harm comes to you. Anyway, you do not have to decide today, I will be here at the same time in two weeks' time and if you would like to come bring a small case with what you will want overnight.'

Janet agreed to this and the two parted good friends. During the next few days Sam wondered what was wrong with his wife. They were both very young and had married very hastily. Now when night came it often brought periods of dreaded avoidance of any kind of proximity on the part of his wife. She had suggested sleeping alone but Sam could not understand how what had seemed to him to be an enjoyable kind of adventure together, or some kind of game, had become something to avoid mentioning. He was a kindly fellow and still very young. He could scarcely believe his luck when the pretty young girl who was staying in the vicinity and was helping to exercise the dogs had spoken to him in a friendly manner and had chosen his company when out coursing. 'Do you work on a farm?' Janet had asked.

'Yes,' Sam had replied shyly. Then, with pride, 'I am in charge of the sheep and we have a good flock. Last year we had a prize for the best average of lambs in the district.'

'How clever,' Janet had replied.

'My boss was presented with a medal at the County Show, and I went. Our pay is not very good you know, if I was married though I could have a cottage.'

'What sort of a cottage?'

'I would have it free and would be much better off, with free milk and any game I could get.'

This had sounded very attractive to Janet, who loved the country, to have a dear little cottage to live in, perhaps with hens and other pets. Nothing to do all day but look after the cottage. She had loved her father but could not bear the thought of sharing him with a new wife, a stepmother. She had agreed to meet Sam on Sunday afternoon and soon a friendship had grown between them. Sam had done all he could to please the girl and although he was sorry that their friendship had gone too far at the time, he had felt convinced when they married that he would be able to make Janet happy. The loss of their child must have really upset her, he came to the conclusion. There was nothing else he could do but be kind to her and hope for the best.

When Janet had first started her married life at the cottage she had been too excited to think any further than the present. The summer was lovely, she could walk in the fields, pick the wild flowers and the long days seemed so peaceful and happy after life with her mother-in-law. Winter, however, had brought cold days and long cold nights. Nothing exciting to do and always the fear of becoming pregnant again. Sometimes her father's words had come back to her. 'If you go ahead with this stupid idea of marrying this fellow, I wash my hands of you. Why you should want to mix with this ignorant country lout I can't think, however, you have made your bed and now you must lie on it.'

His words came home to Janet frequently, she had made a mess of her life. She was sorry for Sam, he worked so hard. The sparcely furnished cottage was uncomfortable and boring. She had soon become tired of its limitations. There was no money for luxuries, in fact hardly enough money to cover the basic requirements of life. The long farm track across the fields to the cottage was often thick with mud which somehow seemed to get everywhere. She grew tired of trying to vary the diet of milk, eggs and potatoes which were the only plentiful free foods available, together with some wild rabbit or bird which was supposed to be partly in lieu of wages. All these things were trying but the worst thing to bear was the hurt look in Sam's eyes when he realized that his love seemed to be rejected. He tried to please, going out of his way to gather wild violets from the shelter of the field hedges, and once he brought home a baby deer he had found crouching motherless in a ditch. The farm was isolated and quite near to parkland. Deer were often surprised by the shepherd dogs and would leap hastily away. Sam had been tempted by the helpless faun and had gathered it up to take home. Janet had appeared delighted and had carefully reared the pretty creature on cow's milk of which they had plenty. The day came eventually when little Billy began to get into mischief. He ate all the young shoots from the small fruit trees and nibbled off the growing vegetables. It was decided eventually that it was best to lose him in the woods where he would find others of his own family and be at home and happy. As the days went slowly by Janet decided that to pass by the opportunity of such an exciting chance outing as that offered by the stranger would be silly, it might never happen again.

She concocted a tale that she would like to go to visit her father and to stay overnight. She explained that she could catch a bus from Warwick and return the same way. Sam was not very happy at the arrangement. He had never met Janet's father but knew that he was despised and looked down upon. Perhaps a visit to see her father would cheer the girl up. He agreed to the visit and encouraged the girl to take a holdall and to wear her best clothes.

It seemed a long wait at the agreed rendezvous. Janet in her excitement had started out much too early and told herself that it was her own fault. She had perched herself on a gate by the roadside to wait. Several cars passed and she began to congratulate herself on having found a way of getting some free entertainment to help to pass the long and boring days. Sooner than she expected a car drew up and Donald's smiling face appeared. 'You decided to come then, I am so pleased.'

Janet climbed into the car and they started off. It was seldom that the girl had the opportunity of riding in a car and it was sheer joy watching the countryside pass. 'Did your people mind your coming?' asked Donald.

'I didn't tell them where I was going or who I was going with,' she replied.

If Donald thought this rather strange he did not say so but congratulated himself on his luck. His wife was a trial sometimes, he did his best to keep her happy but she seemed to grumble at everything he did and said. She took no pride in her appearance and appeared each morning to make breakfast in a dirty wrapper with her grey hair hanging untidily around her face. At best her face was not handsome but the sulky expression did not improve it and she had grown very fat through lack of exercise and fondness of good food. He did not mind what she spent her money on but felt rather guilty at times when other men appeared with their pleasant and attractive wives and he had purposefully refrained from asking his wife to accompany him to any kind of office party or meeting. He hesitated to admit that he was ashamed of her but felt very guilty at what he was about to do. To take a young and attractive girl away with him overnight.

They stopped for a meal at a roadside restaurant and arrived rather late at a large roadside hotel where Donald was immediately recognized. 'Your room is ready sir,' was the welcoming greeting. 'I see you have brought your wife after all.' The porter was instructed to lead the way with the key and to carry the luggage. Donald had brought a small case and Janet hugged the holdall to her chest looking nervously around. She had never stayed at a hotel before and was full of admiration and wonder at the comfortable looking double bed and adjoining dressing room with shower and toilet. She had not given any thought to sleeping with the pleasant stranger. He seemed so kind, almost like her father used to be. She felt sure that he would understand that all she needed was a change of scenery, a nice meal and pleasant company.

'Will you see if you can book two seats for a show this evening.' Janet was surprised when Donald picked up the phone by the bedside and talked to the pleasant lady they had seen at the reception desk. A short time afterwards this telephone rang and Donald was told that seats had been booked for *One night of Love*. He seemed very pleased as he told Janet of their good luck. 'We must go very shortly,' he said, brushing his curly grey hair. Janet hastily examined herself as she looked in the long glass on the mirrored wardrobe. 'Don't worry,' said Donald. 'You look fine. I will get you some chocolates later.'

They both enjoyed the show and had a drink at the bar — Janet did not know what to say when asked what she would like to drink — but something was handed to her which was sweet and made her tongue tingle. She asked for more but was told that it was late and that they had an early start next morning.

Climbing into bed in her prettiest nightgown Janet did not feel at all strange or shy. She cuddled up to her kind friend and allowed all his kisses and wandering hands full play. She was very tired with all that had happened throughout the long day and evening and soon was fast asleep feeling secure in kind enveloping arms.

It seemed no time at all had passed when daylight stole into the room. Donald was fast asleep as Janet looked at him. 'What a nice man,' she thought. 'He has asked nothing of me. He is too good, why did I lie to him? I can't tell him now that I am married, he thinks that I am a lady, a healthy landowner's daughter who rides to hounds.' She felt ashamed and sorry and so full of guilt. Soon Donald was awake and told her to hurry and dress, they must get an early breakfast and start out as soon as possible. He said that he had decided to leave her at the museum for the couple of hours he would have to be away at the firm's head office. He thought that she would find plenty of interesting things there and could get herself a cup of coffee if she liked later.

They arrived back at Janet's farm gate entrance nearing evening and as he said goodbye Donald asked if he could call one day and meet Janet's father. 'Have you told your family about me?' he asked.

'No, they think that I have gone to stay overnight with relatives,' Janet replied.

'What a pity. Never mind, perhaps next time we meet. Give me a kiss, now do you realize that I love you?'

'You are very kind and I like you very much, but what about your wife?'

'We do not need to let her know about our friendship,' replied Donald. 'She has no time for me, if she does not know about our friendship she has nothing to worry about. She has a good home and everything she wants.'

'Except your love,' was on the tip of Janet's tongue but she restrained herself with the thought that her own husband could be said to be in the same position.

That is not true, thought Janet as she made her way across the muddy field road to the cottage. She felt very guilty and tried to think what she would say to all the questions that she was sure to be asked about her father.

Fortunately the house was locked, the key was in its usual

place under an old flower pot near the door and Sam was no doubt away across the fields at work. She had time to replace her nightclothes and to hide the half-eaten chocolates. She hastily prepared a meal, had the table laid and a welcoming warmth in the kitchen of the cottage when Sam came home. There was little conversation. Sam was kind, thinking that his wife looked tired and worried. He pictured stormy rows again between herself and her father and could not really understand why she had voiced a sudden urge to go to see him in the first place. It was difficult for either to start a conversation and at length Sam said, 'You look tired and I didn't get much sleep last night, shall we go to bed early?'

Janet lay beside her sleeping husband for several hours, unable to sleep. She felt miserable and guilty, all kinds of thoughts came and went. Why could she not love and live happily with the man she had married? She had loved him once, or was it that he had been the first boy, other than her brothers, who had spoken to her seriously? He was kind, he thought she was beautiful and told her so. She did not deserve such a kind and loving husband. She resolved at length, when her brain was almost too tired to function, that she would start all over again. She would be kind and good to Sam and be a good and loving wife, but again, when her thoughts turned to the inevitable, the idea of making love, she knew that she could never submit herself to such a sickening experience. 'Only with someone I can love,' she assured herself. 'I am not cold, not heartless, I thought I loved him, he was kind to me, there was no one else. Now I know I do not love him. What shall I do? I do not love Donald either. I cannot see Donald again.' Finally, worn out, she fell asleep.

At six o'clock Sam appeared, fully dressed with a cup of tea as usual. 'How do you feel dear?' he asked. 'You were so tired last night I let you sleep on. I am just setting out with old Nell to go around the sheep. One got herself entangled in some barbed wire yesterday, she will be all right I think.'

'I thought you said old Nell was blind,' replied Janet.

'Yes she is, the vet saw her last week and yesterday he came and said that she is completely blind, yet she can round up the sheep as usual. Of course she has done it on the same land all her life.'

'I still think it is wonderful,' Janet replied, thankful to change the subject and keep the chat away from herself.

3

Days passed and Janet gradually recovered from her feeling of self-reproach. When the time came she decided not to meet Donald and in fact she decided never to meet him again. She tried to be kind to Sam but kept him patiently waiting for some sign that she wished to resume closer relations with him again. Sometimes conversations started during their long lonely evenings about the loving times they had once, how fond they were of each other's company. Then one evening Sam remarked that it was a pity they could not decide to have another child. There would be plenty then to keep them occupied and Janet would have lots to occupy her time. 'Oh, washing nappies I suppose, and getting up at all hours in the night to feed a crying baby. You think that would keep me busy don't you? Well, you never need to look forward to that time, I shall never have another child. I never intend to.' With this angry statement Janet flounced off to bed.

A kind of truce prevailed for the next few days, neither mentioned the subject of babies and each sat reading quietly or looking at the tiny television set they had managed to rent during the few hours they spent together. Janet began to feel pleased with herself and to secretly wish that Sam was aware of her sacrifice in giving up the chance of outings and of an exciting association with someone who appreciated her and who bought her chocolates and took her out in a car.

Spring came and days were longer, Sam was more busy than usual. It was lambing time and he was up very early in the morning and sometimes spent most of the night attending to motherless lambs and sickly sheep. One day Janet found a horrid, slow crawling insect inside her vest when she undressed. She had never seen anything like it before and after killing it took it to show to Sam. 'Oh!' he said, 'I meant to warn you about those, it is a sheep tick. You must be careful to destroy any that you find. I told you not to nurse that lamb the other day. They can be dangerous, their bite is nasty. Keep away from the sheep in future. Fortunately they usually do not live away from the sheep. Soon it will be time to shear and to dip the sheep. There won't be any of these things about then.'

'What about you?' asked Janet, horrified.

'Oh, they don't bother me, I've got used to them I suppose,' replied Sam.

This seemed to be the final straw. The winter had been hard, lonely and cold. It was difficult to get fuel delivered so far from the main road and Sam had been very tired of gathering and sawing up wood for the kitchen range. Now that spring had come at last Janet began to resume daily walks along the road towards the town. She scarcely knew what she hoped for but vainly wished for something to happen. One day a car stopped and a cheeky looking young man asked her if she would like to come for a ride. She looked at his smiling face and knowing eyes and quickly refused. She talked to Sam about trying to get some kind of job for herself. Sam was quite pleased to hear this and said that they could always do with help in the kitchen at the big house. Janet was horrified. Her parents had made an effort to ensure that she had a good education and mention had been made of office work, or some kind of further education. Janet now realized that all this had now been wasted. It was her own fault, she had got herself into this mess and must try to get herself out of it.

One fine afternoon she was walking as she often did along the road toward the town when a car stopped. She had noticed that sometimes a car carried an extra number plate, it had red lettering and she wondered why. This car had an extra one back and front, the driver beckoned her and asked politely if she could tell him how far it was to the next town and if she could recommend a likely place for him to get a late lunch. 'Oh yes,' replied Janet, and mentioned the name of a good restaurant she had noticed when passing. 'I am going into the town,' she said.

'Why don't you accept a lift then?' replied the stranger. 'You are very welcome.'

Janet thought, I wonder if this is Donald over again, but she was soon enlightened when the stranger said, 'I have been to Oxford to collect a new car for a client. I often come, well not perhaps often, sometimes. I have got to sell the car first, I live in Scotland near to Glasgow. Have you ever been there?'

'No,' replied Janet. 'I never go anywhere.' Then, realizing what she had said, she apologized and remarked how nice the interior of the car seemed. It had a faint odour of new leather and looked very comfortable and luxurious. They continued a casual conversation until the town was reached and Janet directed the driver to the restaurant. He then asked if she would like to come in and have lunch with him or at least a cup of coffee if she had already had hers. It would be nice, he said, to talk to someone from this district for a change, he did not often get the chance. Janet had nothing to do that was important and agreed to stay for a cup of coffee whilst he ate. 'One thing that interests me,' Janet asked, 'why do some of the cars that travel along this road have red lettered number plates that do not look permanent?'

'Oh, they are trade plates,' replied the stranger. 'New cars which are collected from the factory in Oxford and are not yet registered to be driven on the road so the firm that has purchased them uses the trade plates to collect the car from the makers. I am taking this car back to Scotland and shall be staying the night on the way.'

Janet was very interested to hear this. She had travelled so little and had a great ambition to learn to drive a car. She informed the stranger, whose name he told her was Will, of her wish. 'Well,' he said, 'I should love to teach you but I shall only be in the district overnight anyway and this car is already sold. The new owner would not be very happy to hear that a learner had been using it.' They both burst out laughing and seemed to have created some kind of a bond together. 'I tell you what,' he then said jokingly, 'You had better come back to Scotland with me for a long holiday, more than one lesson would be required you know.'

Janet laughed. The stranger said, 'I may have to come this way again before very long. How would you like to meet me again one day?'

'Yes, I would like that,' Janet replied and thought that it would give her something to look forward to even if it never happened. I am so sick of my aimless life, she told herself. They talked together through the stranger's meal. 'You are an attractive young lady,' Will said, 'I can't understand what the young men around here are thinking of, haven't you got a regular boyfriend? But I suppose you are only a teenager.'

Janet was taken aback at this unexpected question. She had removed her wedding ring after her first quarrel with Sam and had not replaced it. 'Well,' she prevaricated, 'I have got one or two friends but I prefer an older man, a more experienced one for a regular friend.'

'What about me then? I can drop you a card when I am coming into the district next time, perhaps you would like to meet me.'

Janet was rather taken aback at so frank a reply.

'Perhaps we could spend a weekend together,' continued Will.

'I will think about it,' replied Janet. 'If you do want to write when you are coming this way next time, will you be sure to make it a letter and seal it up?'

'I understand,' said Will. 'There is no need for anyone else to know about your affairs. I will send you a letter in good time, but better still I could telephone you.'

Janet tried to hide her alarm, she could scarcely admit that her family had no telephone, living in the country as they obviously did. 'It would be better if I could phone you,' she said, thinking that she could use the phone box in the village.

'That would be fine, here, I will give you my card and you can reverse the charge if you like.'

Janet looked at the card. Will Pritchard, she read, Garage and Hire Car Proprietor and an address near Glasgow. What a thrill, she thought, I might get a trip to Scotland. They parted, each with a similar thought, that they would meet again and that the future held something exciting.

The next few days seemed more boring than ever before to Janet. She tried to be kind and friendly towards Sam but found herself turning away every time he came near. 'Whatever did I see in him?' she asked herself. 'I must have been mad. Lonely of course. Oh, this horrible backwoods! I would do almost anything to get away from here.' Miserable days passed, time seemed to go so slowly. They scarcely spoke to each other, meals were prepared and eaten in silence. At length the agreed day came for her to telephone her new friend. Sam evinced some surprise when he saw his wife putting on a raincoat and wellington boots to go to the village on what he considered must be an unnecessary visit. He hesitated to ask what the errand could be or offer to go himself. He could not understand what he had done to make his wife such a different girl to the one he had married. He did all he could to make her happy and contented but each day she insisted on walking alone towards the town. Tonight he sat alone waiting for her to return from the village.

Anger which had been smouldering for some time flared up. He put on a heavy coat and set out towards the village. Perhaps he could discover where Janet had been and what for.

Janet eagerly dialled the Glasgow number and was relieved to hear again the familiar voice. 'Hello dear, I have some news for you. I shall be coming to Oxford again next week, I am so glad you phoned, I shall be collecting another car and I have plans for you. How would you like to come back with me for a holiday? I can get accommodation for you at a small guest house near my place of business and can be with you most of the time. You will have a good time, we can tour amongst the lakes, there is lots for you to see. Can you be ready? Just pack a small case and we can buy anything else you might want. I will look out for you at the same place next Tuesday. Don't trouble to make your mind up now. If you are not there I shall decide that you do not want to see me again. Believe me, you would have a wonderful holiday and everyone should go to Scotland once at least.'

Janet said, 'All right, I will try to make my mind up by next Tuesday and if I am not there you will know that I cannot come.'

Janet started for home full of excitement. A holiday in Scotland, how marvellous! She felt that it would be silly to miss this opportunity, it might never come again. What could she say to Sam? It was raining heavily as she turned into the gates and started to tramp across the field road in the mud. It was sometimes the family custom to keep a clean pair of shoes hidden under the small bridge that carried the road over the stream and to change them, leaving the heavy boots under the bridge until the owner returned, but recently someone had found the shoes and had stolen them.

Suddenly Sam appeared, striding through the rain. 'Oh, so you are coming home, are you going to tell me where you have been?'

'No, it's none of your business.'

'Not my business? Have you forgotten that you are my wife?'

'No, unfortunately, you never let me forget. Leave me alone, keep away from me, I am going away next Tuesday.'

'Where to?'

'That's my business.'

The two walked on in silence through the rain and finally came to the cottage door. Janet walked in, took off her wet coat and boots and went straight to bed. Sam was by now quite used to sleeping alone. He could not understand what had gone wrong. He had always thought that Janet was too good for him. He could not understand why she had suddenly taken such a dislike to him but thought it must be the lonely life and lack of money to buy the small luxuries that girls seem to like. He lay awake a long time brooding over the wrong turning that their life seemed to have taken lately. Was it because he had left her alone? But she had turned away from him every time he had tried to get near to her. He began to feel angry, why should he put up with this miserable life, he was working hard and doing his best to make her happy, he didn't drink and didn't knock her about but he had certainly felt like doing so at times. Finally he made a resolve that he would have it out with her, as he termed it, tomorrow.

Next morning they both overslept and after a hurried cup of tea Sam started off across the fields to tend the sheep. Janet got up, replenished the fire and started to prepare breakfast. Tuesday was only three days away, she must make up her mind. What could she tell Sam, why should she tell him anything? She could just leave, but what would happen if Sam did not know where she was? He would probably ask the police to trace her or something equally unpleasant. No, she would have to tell him that she was going away for a holiday with friends. 'What friends?' he was sure to ask. She felt very sorry for him at times but when she tried to console him or to get him to agree to be 'just good friends' he became loving and attempted intimacy. Then a quarrel was again inevitable. She felt resentful against fate that seemed to have guided her path into a pitfall. She had felt so alone after the loss of her mother. She was at home alone so much she had felt happy to find a friend in Sam.

Breakfast was ready when Sam came in and he lingered to talk. 'What are you doing today?' he asked. 'Walking up the road I suppose again. If you want to walk why not try the fields? You might find some mushrooms, and there are violets under the hedge.'

'No, I do not want to walk across the fields today, I have to get my case ready, I shall be leaving on Tuesday for a holiday, I may be away for a week or perhaps longer.'

'Where are you going? I didn't know you had any money for a holiday, I suppose your father gave you some.'

'This will be with friends, you don't know all my friends and these live quite a way away but I shall be back in a week or so. There will be no need for you to have my address, I will let you know later when I shall be coming back.'

Sam grew quite agitated, he started to threaten and stood over her with an arm raised, then his anger melted and began to beg her to stay at home. He was near to tears and Janet began to feel sorry that she had planned to leave him even though it was only for a short time, then she told herself that she must not waver. Why should she not have a holiday? She and Sam together would never be able to save enough money to have a decent holiday, never to go to Scotland anyway. This was a chance not to be missed. She flounced away and went upstairs leaving Sam to finish his breakfast and not returning until he had left the house. She tidied up the kitchen and spent the rest of the day getting her few clothes ready for the holiday. It will be colder in Scotland, she told herself, and added a warm jacket to her collection.

The couple spent the next few days in silence. Each felt afraid to start a conversation, it would certainly lead to another quarrel. On Tuesday morning Janet told Sam that she would be leaving later in the day saying that she would leave his lunch ready. Sam did not reply except to ask when he could expect her back. Janet said she was not sure but expected to be away about a week. 'Perhaps you could bring yourself to let me know when to expect you as soon as you have decided, there will be shopping to do and others might ask where you are.'

4

Janet felt very uncomfortable as Sam walked away across the fields without a backward glance. She continually assured herself as she continued with her packing that she had every right to take a holiday, ignoring her guilty feeling at her deception. She made sure that her bedroom was tidy then set out to walk across the muddy field road to the gate over the stream. She was wearing wellington boots and carrying her best pair of shoes which she intended to put on when she reached the main road. This time she would leave the boots under the bridge and hope that they would be there when she returned.

Janet arrived at the agreed rendezvous well ahead of time with her suitcase and raincoat and an umbrella under her arm. Her friend was late. Janet began as time passed to wish that he would not come at all. She knew that she was doing wrong but an angry feeling of resentment kept returning, and just as she had managed to convince herself that it was perhaps just as well that he was not coming, the car came along and drew up beside her. Will Pritchard was looking eagerly at her as he opened the car door.

Again Janet felt reluctance. A premonition seemed to take possession of her. She told herself that she knew nothing about this fellow's way of life as the car sped on. Surely he had married sometime in his life, he could not be very young. Perhaps his wife had left him or had died. She became more and more worried and then suddenly she said 'Stop.' Will hastily applied the brakes and looked worriedly at her. 'I think I have changed my mind,' Janet said. 'I don't know anything about you really, why are you prepared to give me a holiday? I have nothing to give in return.'

Will looked at her inquiringly, 'Why do you suddenly doubt

me? We were such good friends when we met before, I can assure you that I will look after you and give you a really nice holiday, I have not had one myself lately and you can help me to enjoy this one. It is not very nice trying to take a holiday alone, particularly a travelling holiday.' His tone of voice and his whole manner seemed so warm and friendly, Janet felt the same comfortable trusting feeling that she had felt when in his company before. Somehow Will reminded her of her father when at his most loving and helpful. Before he met his new wife he had been very kind to Janet but it seemed as if he had no time at all for her after he was married.

'How nice the car smells,' remarked Janet, trying to cover her timid feelings.

'Yes. It is the new leather, don't you remember? You remarked on it before.' Soon the uncomfortable feeling passed away and the car moved off to resume their journey.

'I was lucky to get an order for another new car so soon and decided that it was an omen for our good friendship,' said Will. 'I have got a lot to talk to you about. I expect that you realized that I must be a married man. Well, my wife and I have not been happy together for some years now. She came from very far north and has a very narrow outlook on life. She is a good housekeeper and a good and economical cook but a man needs more than that from life, don't you agree?'

Janet felt that she had no right to give an opinion about marriage. She had not told Will that she was married and thought that perhaps this was the time, but could not bring herself to say so. She realized that she would have to do so sooner or later. She knew it would need a very long and detailed explanation to make him understand her position and decided to put it off for the present. He did not seem curious and he had said that he could understand how boring it must be living in such an isolated country place with no opportunity of meeting any suitable friends.

They made good progress and toward evening began to look for suitable accommodation for the night. 'How would you like to go to Blackpool?' Will asked.

Janet could not hide her excitement. 'Oh yes, that would be lovely, I have heard about it but I never even dreamed that I would be able to go there.'

'Well, there is usually plenty of room in small hotels or guest houses,' replied Will.

Janet began to wonder what kind of accommodation Will was looking for. Would she be expected to sleep with him? She was not left long in doubt. Two single rooms were available at the first house that had the magic sign 'Vacancies' outside. They took in their cases, had a wash then strolled out together to see the town. Janet was enthralled. She had never seen anything so wonderful. It was a fine warm evening and they strolled around for a long time. A meal of fish and chips was enjoyed by both, and it was quite late and they were both very tired when they retired for the night.

After an early breakfast they were soon on the road again and Janet grew more and more excited as well-known landmarks that she had heard about were pointed out to her. 'We are now going over Shap pass,' said Will, and later he pointed out Gretna Green and made a short detour to show Janet the famous smithy.

They arrived near Glasgow quite late in the evening and Will lost no time in taking Janet to the small private hotel he had found in the Queen's Park area. It was quite close to his place of business, he said, and promised that he would call for her quite early after breakfast next day. 'I will take you to see my office where I shall have some business to attend to, I hope then to be able to take you out for the day. I will have a lot to tell you, I expect, when I have been home.'

Janet made herself comfortable in the strange bed, marvelling at the spotless cleanliness she saw everywhere and trying to understand the strange accent of the owner. Next morning she enjoyed a hearty breakfast and then began to wonder how she was going to pay for her board whilst she was there. She had brought all her meagre savings with her but they totalled somewhat less than forty pounds altogether.

Promptly Will arrived and escorted her through a back entrance into a well-appointed office which seemed to be at the back of some large garage type premises that were teeming with noise and activity.

'Sit down,' he started. 'I have a lot to tell you. I went home last night to find that my wife had left me. She left a note saying that she had gone to her sister's house in Inverness and did not intend ever to return.'

Janet received this information with mixed feelings. She started to say that she was sorry but Will interrupted her, saying that this was not the first time that his wife had left him. He had travelled all the way to Inverness once when there was snow and very cold weather to try to persuade his wife to return. After a lot of arguing she had finally agreed to try again. 'She had everything she could possibly wish for,' he said, 'I went out of my way to anticipate every whim but there was no satisfying her. As soon as she got one thing she wanted another. She had her own car but had so many accidents that she was banned from driving. She is terribly overweight but makes no effort to control her appetite for sweet things, chocolates and the like. This time I shall not go to fetch her back. I cannot take you to see my home as it might cause talk amongst the neighbours. I don't want to give her any cause to complain. I am sure that she is in touch with the woman next door and will get a full report of my movements.' He took Janet on his knee and kissed her gently. 'Do you think you could grow to care for me?' he asked. 'I know I am very much older than you but I would look after you and if I can get a divorce on the grounds of desertion we could get married.'

Janet tried to hide her dismay at this suggestion. 'I am only here on a holiday you know,' she said.

'Yes I know, dear, but you are a lovely girl, much too nice to live a life without love. I could make you so happy, I would teach you to drive and you would have your own car, I am sure I could make you very happy, we could have wonderful times together.'

Janet was overwhelmed at all this talk but felt very drawn towards this man and began to wonder how she could start to tell him that she was already married. They spent a happy day together. The weather was good and a tour of some of the beautiful countryside was enjoyed and they returned just as the business was closing for the night. Janet sat in the office whilst Will toured the various parts of his works and spoke to his men. Then he came back and sat down again to talk. 'Well,' he said, 'What do you think of my plan? I can rent a small furnished flat for us to share if you like and I am sure that you need not return home for some time. Now, admit to me, you have nothing important to go home for, have you?'

Janet felt bewildered. She could not think how to start to explain. She said 'I haven't brought enough clothes with me to stay very long.'

Will laughed. 'If that's all you are worried about we can go shopping on Monday and buy all you could need for a few weeks anyway.'

'What can I use for money? I have not enough with me to pay for my present hotel bill I am afraid.'

'Don't worry about that, I will take care of that and also buy you anything you need. I am not exactly penniless you know.'

Janet felt very tempted and said to herself, 'Why not? I shall never get a chance like this again.'

'Perhaps I can stay for a bit longer then,' she replied.

'There's no time like the present,' said Will. 'I think I know where there is a nice furnished flat, I will take it for a month, that will give us breathing space.'

Without further delay they set off in the car to a small village near Kilmarnock and Will rang the bell of a clean looking cottage and a lady came at once to the door. 'You advertised a furnished flat?' Will said.

'Yes, would you like to see it?' She took a key from a hook near the door. 'It is really part of this bungalow and is quite private,' she said as she opened the door and ushered them in. 'You could use the garage and there is linen if you wish.' She continued to show them around the flat and Janet thought how lovely it looked. 'The flat is to let on a monthly tenancy only, the owner is abroad for six months.'

'We would like to take it for a month to start with, if that is convenient, and we could move in at once.'

A rent was agreed and Will said, 'There you are, all we have to do is to stock the larder and you can go ahead and act the housewife.'

'I thought you said that we were going on holiday.'

'Yes, of course, but I have to get my clothes and other personal things over here from the house, you can have your clothes here too. When we have it all neat and tidy we can start our holiday from here.'

'Where shall we go?' asked Janet.

'I have a good man I can leave in charge and if you like we can tour the Highlands, what about the Loch Ness Monster? Would you like to go looking for that?'

Janet thought everything was progressing too fast. She felt a kind of fascination for this sophisticated yet kind and affectionate stranger. It seemed obvious that she would be expected to share his bed, all they had shared up to the present had been a warm, affectionate kiss. Strangely she felt no objection to the idea, she even felt a kind of tingle of excitement. She kept putting away from her mind all thoughts of her old life. She felt a new, different and exciting person. She seemed to have strayed into another world, a different world, a world of excitement. Something she had never felt before. They seemed to find each other warm, friendly and comfortable to be with. Janet had a comforting feeling that she was being taken care of. That there was nothing to fear.

They sorted out sheets and blankets and made up a bed which they shared, finding a new and thrilling experience together. Janet thought, 'Is this really love?' If this was love she had never felt anything like it before. Something that she had previously thought was a dream world, a dream world that never really exists, except in story books. Here it was, really happening. Will also wondered what had happened to his sane and ordinary life, his everyday marriage that had become so boring. He had found a delightful, warm, loving companion. One who opened her eyes wide in wonder at places that previously had seemed to him quite ordinary. She saw and remarked upon things that had been accepted as not just ordinary but sometimes almost objectionable. Strangely she saw and could point out something of interest or of beauty, even wonder at everyday occurrences. It was to Will a wonderful experience to just stroke the soft, warm, loving girl beside him, to experience the delight of her soft warm kisses and wide wondering eyes. He felt young and excited all over again. If he could only marry this girl and have her with him always. Ida had left him, not for the first time, he would ask for a divorce.

5

They had a wonderful holiday, Will knew all the wonderful places to visit. Janet said that she enjoyed most of all the ride on the ferry from Gourock. Life now was to her a glorious dream come true. One day a new thought occurred to her. She suddenly became very concerned. Suppose she became pregnant? Next day she told Will that she really should return home. She had already been away longer than the original week that she had spoken about to Sam. He would be wondering where she was and might start some inquiries. That night, safe and warm in Will's comforting arms, she voiced her question, was she likely to become pregnant?

'Oh no,' replied Will. 'Leave that to me.'

'But I should be returning home soon now.'

Then Will told her of his plans. 'I love you, Janet, and I want to make you my wife. I have written to my wife and have asked her to divorce me. If I don't get a reply soon I will telephone her. She cannot expect me to continue with what is no marriage at all, and has not been a true marriage for a very long time.'

Janet felt speechless. Will continued, 'It is time that she set me free to have a chance of happiness with someone else, someone who returns my love. Tomorrow I will take you to look at a house that is being built near here. It is almost finished and I would like to buy it as soon as my wife agrees to set me free. Then I will sell my old house and you and I can live in the new one. I will take you to see it today, but don't you think you should let your family know where you are and what you are planning to do? You love me, don't you, and you would like to be my wife? We could have a glorious time together. I promise that I will teach you to drive and you can have a little car of your own.'

Janet knew that she must write to Sam but could not give him her address. Then she had an idea. She could give him the address of the post office and then she could collect any reply he might send. She would call in at the one just down the road the next time that Will had to go to his business. She would make an arrangement with them that she would collect any reply that came for her. She sat down quietly to write as soon as she was alone. She was living in the present and did not stop to think how she would feel when the brief holiday was over and Will had to return to full-time at the office. Suppose he went down to Oxford to fetch another car? How could she bear to be left alone??this strange place where she knew no one at all? She composed a short letter saying that she was staying for a little while longer with her friends and if Sam wanted to write back he could address it care of the post office. She then took a short walk down to the shops, posted the letter and bought some bread. Then she went to see the postmistress and said that she was only staying for a short time in the district, would they mind if she gave a poste restante address to a friend and called later to collect any letter that might come? She was not sure where she might be for some days ahead. The postmistress was very helpful and said that she would keep any letter that arrived. Having left her name, Janet left the post office and quickly walked back to the flat. She just had time to clear away the remains of breakfast and tidy up before Will arrived, full of excitement. He had permission to view the new house that was just finished, on a very attractive site with trees and a stream nearby. They were both very excited and found the house to be just what they had visualized. Janet fell in love with it at once and thought how she could make it attractive and be happy there. She put aside all ideas of returning to live with Sam but could think no further than the immediate future. Will had not got any agreement about his divorce yet. He talked very little on that subject and Janet wondered if his wife had failed to agree. She tentatively asked Will if he had received any news from his wife, knowing that a letter would be sent to his office or to his old home that she had never seen.

'No,' replied Will. 'I have told her that I shall put the house on the market tomorrow. It will find a customer very quickly, in fact I already know several people that are interested. We can have the furniture brought to our new house as soon as the purchase details are settled. We can measure for carpets immediately if you like and then we can go into town and look at some. There is a small amount of decorating still to be done and we will call in and decide a colour scheme, if you like, in a day or two.'

Janet was delighted with this information but right in the back of her mind, where she had continually pushed the thought that she would have to come out into the open about her marriage or she would find herself faced with bigamy, the nagging worry kept returning. Then suddenly Will asked, 'Have you told your family that you are going to stay on here yet?'

'No,' replied Janet, 'I can't write really, I don't know what to say.'

'I must admit that I don't understand why you can't tell them that you have met a friend and that you will be staying here for a period and have found a friend who might like to marry you, or something to that effect. Have you thought what a sudden shock it might be to your father to hear your news after not being kept in the picture at all?'

'I am not interested in what my father would feel,' replied Janet quickly. 'He has told me that now he has married again he does not want anything to do with me.' Janet then realized that she had thoughtlessly said too much and began to worry about Will's reaction.

However, he just said, 'Well I suppose you know what you are doing, as long as I don't have to be faced by an irate father some time in the future I don't mind.'

'There's no fear of that,' replied Janet.

* * *

'Get your coat on, you are going to have your first driving lesson today,' said Will. 'I have brought a set of L-plates with me.'

The two had another enjoyable day together. Janet had her lesson and was complimented on her road sense. She felt full of joy that she had found such a happy life and such a marvellous companion. She put away all misgivings about the future and enjoyed every moment of her life. If she did allow herself to think at all it was with a smouldering feeling of resentment that began to slowly build in her mind. She did not look upon herself as having been silly in doing wrong with Sam, she blamed him for everything in her mind. How could he expect her to live in that badly furnished, isolated cottage for the rest of her life? When she had suggested getting for herself some kind of employment he had suggested housework. She thought sometimes of her schoolfriend that she had stayed with in that lovely old manor farmhouse near to the cottage. She had never dared to approach her friend again. She was so ashamed of her surroundings. Her friend was probably still at school. She had stated in her letter to Sam that she was staying on in Scotland for a while longer, and wondered if she should write again and ask for a divorce. She had no idea at all how these things were managed and second thoughts said wait for a while and see how Will goes about it.

Several days later Janet found herself alone for a while and hurried along to the post office to see if a reply had been received to her letter to Sam. Yes, there was a letter. She did not stop to read it but hurried home in case Will returned before her. It was Saturday, the last day of Will's holiday, and Janet thought she would have much more time to answer the letter, if it required an answer, next week when she was alone in the house. She went to the bathroom and bolted the door, taking out the letter with trepidation she started to read. The colour spread slowly over her face, she could imagine that the letter was stained with dried tears.

'How could you stay away from me so long? I love you, we are pals. Have you forgotten everything? I have always tried to be kind to you. Where did you get the money to go on holiday? Who is paying for it? Why must I be a box number? Are you ashamed of your friend's attitude to me, your husband? When can I expect you home?'

The letter started with anger and ended with sorrow. Janet could not think what to reply. She hastily stuffed the letter behind a jar of bath salts in the cupboard as she heard Will entering the house. She could not bring herself to destroy it until she had read it again.

They spent the afternoon at a football match. Janet had never been to anything like this one. She had seen local boys playing in a very amateurish way occasionally but this was the famous Queens Park. They went home to tea and the evening was spent at the Glasgow Empire Theatre where variety was on the stage.

Janet still felt in a dream world. She decided that she would try to answer Sam's letter on Monday. They paid the new house another visit on Sunday and began to plan just where the furniture would go.

'If my wife will not agree for me to sell the house I may have to sell my shop,' said Will. 'You do not know about my shop yet, I hesitated to tell you because so many people look down on the trade. It is called a "Fish Supper Shop". It is only open evenings and is run for me by a woman.'

'Oh, can I go to see it?' asked Janet. 'I know about fish and chip shops, we have them you know.'

'You might be disappointed,' replied Will. 'This is not a fish and chip shop, all that is sold is a packed meal in a box. People usually place a regular order and call for their boxes. Do you like fish and chips?'

'Yes, of course,' Janet replied.

'It's a bit difficult for me to take you to see the shop because my wife has visited it. In fact she managed it whilst Fanny, that's my woman in charge's name, had a holiday last spring.'

'Oh, perhaps I shall be able to do that now,' said Janet excitedly.

'You would not like it you know, the smell gets everywhere. Into all your clothes and even into your skin.'

'I could have a bath.'

'You have no idea, have you? Even a bath does not completely remove the odour.'

They let the subject drop and Janet began to worry about the letter hidden in the bathroom, she had not yet had an opportunity to destroy it and when Will said he was going to have a bath she suddenly remembered it. He appeared with the letter in his hand. 'Who is Sam?' he asked. 'How could you deceive me? Why not give this address?'

Janet broke down and sobbed out the full story. Will took her on his knee and tried to comfort her. 'You silly girl,' he said. 'Why not tell me for a start that you were married. This changes the situation. It's no use my getting a divorce, I can't marry you unless you are free, and it does not look by the tone of this letter that you have any chance of getting free. How could you treat the poor chap like that? It looks heartless to me, don't you love him? If not why did you marry him?'

Janet hesitated to tell him the truth and said that she didn't really know but that she had felt so lonely.

'Are you going to reply to the letter and give this address?' Will asked.

Janet looked frightened. 'I will reply and say that I am not coming back and I will tell him to forget me,' she replied.

After a while the episode was temporarily forgotten and Will decided to sell his fish supper shop. To his surprise Fanny said that she would like to take over the shop. Janet expected this would be good news but Will said that he was afraid that Fanny did not have immediate capital available, however if she could find the money it would solve some of their difficulties. Nothing more was said for some days. Will had resumed his place as managing director of his business but Janet found that he was liable to walk into the flat at any time of the day. A date had been arranged for settlement and possession of the new house and Janet looked forward to a busy time ahead. There was a small garden to be planned and there would be much to do once he house was taken over and the furniture had arrived. Will took Janet to measure the windows and to a well-known shop to choose curtains. He said that he would also have to choose carpets as it would be best to leave the others at the old house for the purchaser. Janet felt rather annoyed that she could not see the house but Will was firm in his refusal to visit. He said that he would go one day and pack up anything there that his wife would look upon as personal and send it to her. He had not obtained her consent to a divorce as yet and in the light of his discovery that Janet was also married he decided not to press the matter at the moment.

The first time Janet found herself alone in the flat she set off to the post office to see if there was any further mail for her. She wondered what would happen to any letter that was waiting there for her if she did not call and she felt a little apprehensive in case someone had made it their business to discover where she lived. She entered the shop and the postmistress immediately beckoned her over to a corner and lifting a part of the counter invited her into the rear of the shop. 'Your husband was here on Saturday,' she said. 'At least he said he was your husband and he wanted to know where you lived. I managed to convince him that I did not know and that it was no use waiting as it might be several days before you called her again. The poor fellow was distracted. I felt so sorry for him, will you promise me that you will let him know where you are? At least write. Why not go back to him? I know it is none of my business but he seemed such a nice man and he said that he had travelled overnight by train and that he had decided to come in a hurry and could not stay because of his job.'

'Yes, I understand and thank you,' replied Janet, and walked out of the shop trembling with shock and fear.

She was still trembling with fear and worry when Will came home. She had made no effort to get a meal ready and the full realization of what she had done began to make itself felt. Will wanted to know what had happened and she stammered out the truth. 'You are a silly girl,' he said. 'Why didn't you tell me the truth in the first place? I should never have brought you here. You said there was no one to care where you went and now it seems that you have a husband who is willing to travel all this way by train and to forgive you and to take you back. You are a very lucky girl you know.'

Janet was so shaken with the fear that Will would send her home that she clung to him hysterically. Will began to fear that he had trouble on his hands. 'I don't know what I can do with you, I have literally bought a house, asked my wife for a divorce, put my shop on the market, and amongst other things I cannot very well recall that letter I sent to my wife.'

'Oh please do not send me back,' sobbed Janet. 'I love you and want to stay here, I do not love my husband and I can ask him to divorce me.'

Will could not help feeling sorry for the wretched girl and took her in his arms. 'All right, you can stay but write a letter at once to your husband telling him this address. If what you say about his circumstances is true he will not be very likely to travel here again. In any case we can go to the house as soon as I can get furniture delivered there.'

'Have you heard from your wife about the divorce yet?' asked Janet.

'No, and I shall be surprised if she agrees to it, she loves me in her way. I must admit I did rather fall for you and thought it might be easy to start life again but in the light of this new information I am not sure if it is the best thing to do.'

'What do you mean?' asked Janet. 'Surely you don't mean to pack me off back home?'

'No, you can stay here, I still love you, you silly little goose, but you must get things straight with that husband of yours. I don't want to get labelled a wife stealer.'

'Oh yes, I will,' replied Janet hurriedly. 'I will write at once and make things clear.'

A kind of truce was achieved and at length the day came to move into the new house and Janet was very excited. They unpacked all the furniture together and decided where each thing should go. The new carpet had been laid and the curtains hung. Janet felt tired but so pleased when the time came to spend her first night in the new home. 'What shall we call the house?' she asked.

'Just No 11,' Will replied.

'Oh, that's much too ordinary.' Janet dared not say that her only home since she married had been a tied cottage on a farm. 'Can't we call it Newholme or Journey's End?' she asked.

'No,' replied Will. 'I flatly refuse to call it any fancy name. No 11 it is and it shall stay at that.'

This new definite mood that Will was in rather frightened Janet. He had been so kind and loving. Why was he different? He seemed cold and felt somehow as if he was a different person. He was not now the gentle, loving, fatherly man that she had got used to. He made no offer to take her in his arms and as days went by they seemed to be no more than just friends. I blame Sam for all this, she told herself angrily, why did he have to come here interfering? I don't worry him or care what he does, why should he try to order my life for me? I shall never, never go back to him.

Janet little knew that Will had been in conversation with his wife on the telephone, and that she had expressed her willingness to come back to him. He realized how he missed her clever cooking, she knew just what he liked. The house was always clean and comfortable and, more important still, she never enquired where he was going or asked where he had been. After all, life might be rather dull with her as company but at least there had been no harassment or worry when his wife had been in charge of the house.

6

Janet tried to settle down in her new house and became rather friendly with the wife next door. The two met for coffee on alternate mornings when they were both at home alone. Jean's husband was a commercial traveller and almost always away all the week, returning on Friday evening. They had one small boy and spent weekends in the country quite often during the nice weather. One day the two friends were having coffee together. It was Monday and Will had gone to the office and Jean's husband had started out on a journey to England to make his usual calls. 'Look what I had for a present on Saturday,' said Jean, producing a jewel case containing a very nice looking pearl necklace.

'Oh how lovely!' exclaimed Janet. 'Is it your birthday or something?'

'No,' replied Jean, 'but I know why he has given it to me,' and a faraway look came over her face.

'Why then?' asked Janet.

'Don't you know?'

'Of course I don't know. How could I?'

'Your husband goes away overnight sometimes doesn't he?' asked Jean.

'Yes, but I don't see how that merits a gift.'

'Think again, you don't ask him where he has been and what he has been doing all those nights away from home, do you?' said Jean. 'How do you know who he spends his time with?'

'Oh, I am sure Will would not deceive me,' said Janet, horrified at the thought.

'That's what you think, all men are the same, but they are simple really, you would think they would realize that it rather gives them away when they feel so guilty that they have to bring a gift home. That makes them feel better, you see, I have known about this for a long time but there is nothing one can do about it so one is well advised to make the best of it and not look a gift horse in the mouth as the saying goes.'

Janet felt quite shocked at this disclosure and started to wonder if she would have a gift next time Will had occasion to go to Oxford to fetch a new car. Then she felt ashamed of the thought, why should she think that she could not trust him? Then again her busy brain went on, what about the time he had spent away from home with her? What did he tell his wife then? Of course, she told herself, he was not sleeping with his wife then and I don't suppose she cared where he had been when he was away from her. All the same, Janet began to realize that life might not be quite so rosy here as she had at first thought.

But I couldn't go back to Sam, she told herself with horror. It would be 'I told you so' all the time. Life was bad enough there before, what would it be now? He would have plenty to taunt me about and I expect he has told everyone he knows his side of the story.

Janet tried to tell herself that life was just the same, that Will still cared for her and was planning their life together, nevertheless when he was away overnight she spent a sleepless night wondering what he was doing. She must make herself attractive and fascinating for him when he returned.

Some weeks elapsed. The autumn chill was in the air. Janet realized that she now lived very much farther north then before and could expect cold weather sooner, a less warm summer and a longer winter and a more severe one. The thought was depressing and when one day Will announced that he had to go to Oxford to collect another new car she secretly hoped that he would suggest taking her with him. Her driving was improving and although she had not yet passed her driving test the time was getting near.

The last night came before Will was due to start for Oxford. They retired early and Janet put on her loveliest négligé, told Will how much she loved him and would miss him. She curled up near to him in bed and said, 'Will you miss me tomorrow night?' trying hard to resist saying 'Take me with you.'

Will seemed, she thought, almost indifferent. 'Of course I will miss you. Don't keep me awake talking so silly, I want to be away early. If you want something to do you can get up and make a packet of sandwiches up for me and a flask of coffee.'

How can he think of such mundane things when I am sad and depressed at being left alone?

'What are you worrying about?' said Will. 'If you are lonely you can go next door for a few hours tomorrow evening and then you could go shopping, you like shopping.'

'Not without you,' replied Janet.

'Don't be such a baby, you know your way about now, you can take a bus from the corner, spend the day shopping, have lunch at Simpsons. You've got some money haven't you?' Will was getting impatient and, pushing her away said, 'For goodness sake go to sleep.'

Janet lay awake for many hours. I suppose he's tired of me now, she thought, and rose early, spending a long time making up tasty sandwiches. Will said a casual goodbye, looking worried, and started off early. Janet spent a long time cleaning and re-arranging the items one by one in the house. She tried to feel comfort from the thought that it was her home to live in and enjoy, that she would one day be able to remarry and have a husband that she could love and respect. In spite of all her efforts to cheer herself up the depressing thought kept returning. She did not have a loving husband yet, and might never have Will for a husband. The home was not hers, it was hers only as long as she could make herself happy to live in it. The day seemed long and the night seemed longer. At first she had decided that she would not go to bed because she would not be able to sleep. She tried to pass the time watching television and then reading a book but the night seemed to last for ever.

Eventually she felt ill and lonely as daylight dawned. She knew that she would be welcome next door but did not feel like listening to her friend's cheerful chat. How could Jean be so cheerful? She knew her husband amused himself with other women yet she was content to forget all about this and behave as if it never happened, just to be sure of a nice home and money to spend as she wished. How could she? Am I the only woman who can't live happily without love? she asked herself. Is this one time that I have met a man I can really love to end in unhappiness? Where can I go if I leave here? I will have to leave if he does not want me. The thought that he could be with some other woman — even casually — was heartbreak to her.

The day dragged on and in the early evening Will suddenly

appeared, bright and cheerful as usual. 'How have you been?' he started.

Janet was taken by surprise and knew that she appeared at her worst, her hair was rough and untidy, her face swollen with tears. 'How do you think?' she snapped. 'You go off and leave me here all alone, in a strange place amongst people I don't know.'

'That will do,' replied Will. 'I am tired, I have driven a long way and have hurried home, driving faster than I should have done with a new car because I knew you were alone, and this is what I get. I pictured at least a welcome, a cheerful face and perhaps signs that a nice meal was not far away. It's a pity I did not stay away another night, at least I could have found cheerful company.'

'Like the company you have been with I suppose,' replied Janet. 'Don't forget I know how you go about it.'

'Well, I couldn't be sure of finding anyone quite so eager again could I?' returned Will. Immediately he had fired this remark at Janet he could see that he had gone too far. The girl looked overwrought, in fact almost ill. She really did miss me, he thought, what a fool I have been. I could quite easily have taken her with me, never mind, she will get over it I suppose. Will was not used to such a violent reaction. He had formed several casual relationships over the long years of his marriage. Not because he was dissatisfied with his marriage but partly out of boredom. If an opportunity for a mild flirtation occurred he usually enjoyed a mild fling, assuring the girl that he was happily married and that his wife was away or some such excuse. He realized that when he met Janet he had felt entirely different, partly he suspected because his wife was not at home and he felt neglected. He tried to analyse his feelings for Janet. It was almost an unforgiveable blow that she had dealt him in keeping the fact of her own marriage secret. He had let his mind wander along a star-filled path. Wild dreams of a perfect life of love and happiness with a young impressionable girl who seemed delighted with his every move and was not slow in telling him how much she loved him, but was this kind of love the kind he desired?

Life had been smooth and trouble free for many years, if not exciting. Did he think the thrill of a new love was worth the penalty of having to account for his every move?

At length each decided that they were on dangerous ground and could be capable of going too far in the anger of the moment. They fell asleep in each other's arms and when morning came all too soon, Will had to leave early and Janet was again alone. She spent most of the morning planning an attractive meal and determined to have a frank discussion at the first opportunity about the prospect of Will's divorce and to suggest that as Sam had not replied to her letters she should perhaps make the journey to go to see him and to demand that he give her a divorce forthwith. She felt that as a married and settled woman she could more easily bear the separations that were inevitable when Will left to collect a new car, or for any other business. Lunch time came and Will appeared with a large bunch of flowers. They enjoyed the meal and Will suggested a drive into the country. He had a client to see and could take Janet with him. She was delighted and donned a pair of easy fitting slacks saying that she would like to drive. Her test had been fixed for the following Monday and she was anxious to get in as much practice as possible. They enjoyed the afternoon together, called at a wayside cafe for a cup of tea and arrived home feeling that life was very good.

During the evening Janet ventured to ask Will if he had heard from his wife. He looked away. Should he tell Janet of the letter he had destroyed at the office? The letter which read never, never, never, would she agree to a divorce. 'No,' he said, 'but it's not much use my getting free if you are still married, is it?'

'I want to talk to you about that,' Janet said. 'I thought perhaps that if I passed my test next week I could drive down to see Sam and tell him that I want him to divorce me.'

Will looked a bit surprised. 'We will see about that when you have passed your test,' he said. 'There is a small car in the garage that is for sale, it is not up to date but quite serviceable, a clean dependable little job, we will have to see about it when you have passed.'

'I feel quite confident, and you said yourself that you felt quite happy with me in the driving seat.'

'Yes, I think you will pass all right but don't get too confident, we shall see.'

There was plenty to do at the new house, the garden was still very rough and some shrubs had arrived that should be planted. A load of tiny pebbles was expected to arrive for the small drive in front of the house and it would be quite a job to rake them down and to make them smooth when they arrived. They both worked quite hard over the weekend and there was little time for lovemaking or for any further discussion about the future.

Janet went to her test appointment confidently on Monday and quite easily passed. There was excitement and celebration in the evening. Janet was not used to alcohol and Will forgot that fact and refilled her glass several times. They both retired somewhat mixed up but very happy. Next morning there was the usual hurried rush for bathroom, breakfast and an early start for the office for Will. Janet was left to spend the morning tidying up the house and preparing lunch. This is not quite the life I would have chosen, she thought to herself, but after all there was a lot to be thankful for. A nice home, plenty of time to spend as she wished and apparently no shortage of money. When Will comes home, she told herself, I will ask about the car I am to have. Then I shall be able to go for a drive any time I like and I can go to see Sam and find out why he does not answer my letters. I don't know how long it takes to get a divorce but the sooner it is started the better.

When Will arrived, late as usual for his lunch, she started the conversation by asking when she could have the car he had spoken about. 'I am not too sure about the brakes,' he said. 'I feel it would be better if it has an overhaul before you take it over. After all, you are a beginner and I would never forgive myself if you started out on a long journey in a car that was not absolutely reliable.'

'Can't you get someone to look at it this afternoon?' asked Janet.

'Yes, I suppose so, when do you want to set out on your journey to the Midlands?'

'As soon as possible, you say that I must get my divorce started first so it seems as if I shall have to go to see Sam about it. He does not reply to my letters and it is no use waiting and waiting.'

'All right, I will put a chap on it this afternoon.'

Will went back to the office and called in the young mechanic who had recently started working for the firm and said, 'I want you to look over that Mini in the corner and check the brakes, I have a customer for it tomorrow and I want to be sure it is roadworthy.'

'It's a good little job, boss,' said the lad, 'but I will check it over and have it ready for you tomorrow morning.'

When Will told Janet that the car would be ready for her tomorrow Janet was delighted and spent time packing some clothes for an overnight stay. 'There's no hurry for you to return you know,' said Will. 'It is a long journey and you will be glad of a day's rest when you get there, you are not an experienced driver yet, you know, and there is no great hurry. Have you got money?'

'Yes I have some money but not much, I shall need money for the return journey.'

Will gave her money for her needs and took her with him next day to the garage. They arrived very early and Janet could not wait to get started. 'I must see the report the mechanic has left first,' said Will. The young fellow had not yet arrived but had left a note to say that he could find nothing wrong with the car and had checked and inflated the tyres, checked water, oil etc. Will filled the petrol tank and Janet set out on her long journey delightedly. 'You can telephone me tomorrow if you can and tell me how things are,' said Will as she started off. It was a long journey and the first that Janet had undertaken by herself, it seemed to her quite straightforward. She had mapped out the route for herself and as mile after mile was covered the little car seemed easy to handle, and after a call at a Little Chef restaurant for a quick lunch she began to hope that she might reach her destination before too late in the evening.

She had not notified Sam that she was on her way deliberately as she wished to take him by surprise but as the day passed she began to realize that it would be very late when she arrived at the cottage and that Sam would most certainly have gone to bed.

She was not willing to spend any of her precious money on accommodation for the night. She had not liked asking Will for money and hoped to be able to manage on what she had. Then she missed a sign and realized that she must be on the wrong road. She decided to ask a well-dressed man if she was on the right road for Derby. To her surprise and annoyance he opened the car door and got in beside her. 'I will direct you, that is where I am going,' he said. 'Do you intend to spend the evening there? You are obviously a stranger in this district.'

Janet was trembling with fear and could scarcely speak. 'No, I am visiting friends,' she finally replied.

'Where exactly?' he asked.

Janet felt even more alarmed and said, 'I believe there is a bypass, I wish to avoid the town. I will put you down there.'

'That's all right, I have plenty of time, I would have caught a bus anyway if you had not come along.'

Soon they came to a roundabout and directions were clear. 'You can get out now,' said Janet. 'I know the way now.' A great feeling of relief spread through her muscles and she began to breath naturally again as the car sped along. 'That was a risky thing to do,' she told herself and resolved never to do it again.

* * *

Soon she began to recognize landmarks as she drew nearer to her erstwhile home and it was after midnight as she passed from the road to the muddy farm drive, skirted the farmhouse and travelled over the bumpy track to the cottage. She stopped the car with difficulty. She had noticed that the footbrake did not seem to be working very well, the car had taken some time to come to a stop when the man had wanted to leave and it seemed worse now. She placed a stone that was handy under the wheel and made sure the handbrake was tight and made her way to the cottage door. All was quiet, even the farm sheepdog stood up by his kennel and wagged his tail in recognition. The guinea fowl that usually roosted in the trees nearby, and often made a great noise if they thought strangers were about, remained silent.

She suddenly annoyed herself by feeling reluctant to knock on the door. She felt afraid that Sam would be very angry, for one thing her unexpected arrival would anger him, but he had no telephone and she had no wish to acquaint any other person with their private affairs. She wondered how much Sam had discussed with his employers. He knew no one else at least on an intimate footing and was naturally a taciturn man. There was no response to her timid knock and she then raised the old-fashioned, heavy iron knocker and let it drop heavily. The noise seemed to rock the house. The dog started to bark, a flock of pigeons that were roosting on the roof in the shelter of the large chimney took flight noisily and alighted on the ground, curiosity overcoming their fear. Suddenly a bedroom window opened and

Sam called out, 'Who is there?'

'It's me, come on down and let me in.'

'What a time of night to arrive home,' muttered Sam as he angrily unbolted the door. 'How did you get here? Whose car is that?' said Sam, peering round the door and staring at the car.

'It's mine, let me in for goodness sake.'

The two sat down in the still warm kitchen, Janet poked up the fire, added a handful of sticks and put the kettle on.

'I suppose you think you can use this place as a hotel and come go as you like now,' grumbled Sam.

'It's my home as well as yours,' replied Janet and set about making some tea.

'It's too late now to talk and I have to be up early in the morning. I am busy ploughing and have left the tractor at the edge of the field near the river. I have only got about three hours sleep before I have to start again as soon as it gets light.' Janet poured herself a much needed cup of tea and whilst Sam disappeared upstairs she gathered up a rug and settled herself on the old kitchen settle with a hard cushion for a pillow and thankfully settled to sleep.

She was rudely awakened when Sam came down as daylight began to enter the window and poked the fire, starting the dull embers into flame and adding more sticks. 'Well, what have you got to say for yourself?'

'I want a divorce,' answered Janet flatly.

'What? What sort of fool do you take me for? You walk in and out as you please, go off with someone else and think you can come back here and expect me to do just what you want, no fear, not likely.'

Sam hovered over her with blazing eyes. Janet had never seen Sam in a temper before. He had a large chopper in his hand which he was using to split the wood to kindle the flames. He looked threatening and Janet suddenly realized that she had placed herself in some danger. Sam was obviously half out of his mind and the chopper looked deadly. Looking around she suddenly saw the large heavy iron poker standing up by the fireside. She grasped it and shouted, 'Put that thing down and talk sensibly.' She felt half fear and half exasperation. 'I want a divorce I tell you, you might as well agree and get it over with.'

'I'd rather see you dead at my feet,' shouted Sam.

Janet grasped the poker and as Sam raised the chopper and

picked up a piece of wood, she aimed at his head. Fortunately the blow fell short but it seemed to bring her to her senses. 'I can't live here in this horrible lonely place, pinching and scraping all the time to make ends meet, wearing other people's old clothes.'

'It doesn't look as if you are very hard up,' replied Sam. 'You say the car outside is yours, what did you do to get that off your fancy man?'

Janet began to feel her own temper take possession of her as Sam stood over her, chopper in hand, with blazing eyes. She was convinced that he meant to attack her with it. There was no room to get away in the tiny kitchen, Sam blocked the way as he stood threateningly over her. Panicking, she again swung the heavy poker and felt it contact with a dull thud. Sam's eyes seemed to droop as he staggered and fell against the wooden settle. He lay quite still, blood began to well from the wound in his head made by the poker.

Janet felt cold fear steal over her in place of the hot anger that had robbed her of any sense of caution. She dropped the poker and tried to examine the open wound. She tried to make him speak. He lay silent. She tried to feel his pulse but was unaware of any movement. Then panic took possession of her. She listened for a while. There was no sound apart from the call of birds waking up to greet the dawn.

She tried again to awaken the lifeless looking man. His eyes were half-open and seemed fixed and frightening in their cold stare. Suddenly she took a hasty decision and started to drag the heavy body across the kitchen and out of the door. The dog was waiting by his kennel and started to wag his tail again in greeting, then, looking at the recumbent figure, a look of fear passed over his intelligent face and he began to whine.

Purposefully Janet began to drag the body through the garden gate and across the half-ploughed field to the tractor standing facing the river bank. I wonder how you start this thing, she asked herself, and started to examine the controls. She could see nothing that made any sense to her but the stubborn sense of purpose that was within her made her persevere. It was hopeless. Never could one expect to see a piece of road travelling machinery less like her small Mini car where the controls were concerned. Then, walking round the huge mud covered wheels, she noticed that a back wheel was carefully blocked with a large lump of heavy wet wood. She could see that the tractor was at the very top of the slope and pictured how it could gain momentum and career out of control down into the river. She had heard Sam say how dangerous that end of the wheatfield was being so near the river bank.

She felt very angry and very afraid. Her sense of purpose drove her with added strength to heave the blocks and one by one she was able to remove them. Hastening to the inert body of her husband she lifted it up and placed it in the seat of the tractor, then, kicking away the last block, it took all her will power and strength to start the heavy machine gently moving over the edge of the slope and down towards the river, gaining momentum as it went. With a mighty splash it sank into the deep mud of the deeper looking water. Soon only a part of it was visible. Janet heaved a huge sigh of relief and horror mixed together. What had she done! What had taken possession of her? First of all fear that Sam was going to attack her. 'I was only defending myself, he was going to hit me with that chopper.' Deep down in her heart a small voice said, 'You know he would never have harmed you, he loved you.' What shall I do now, she thought, I must get back to the house and go away quickly. Suddenly she remembered that the car was not in driving condition. Those brakes, she thought, I shall have to get them put right, the car is dangerous, what shall I do?

She went back to the cottage and tried to drink a cup of tea but it seemed impossible to swallow it. She sat down to think. I must walk to the village and telephone Will, she decided. He will tell me what to do. She cast an eye on the useless car, locked up the cottage, then unlocked it again. Sam never locked the door in daytime. The dog began to whine and she let him loose. I suppose I should feed him. She went to find something for him to eat in the small pantry. Leaving the cottage with the dog inside she set out for the village. It was about eight am when she arrived at the familiar phone box and she hurriedly dialled her own home number. Will would be having his breakfast, she thought, and waited anxiously, thoughts flitting through her brain.

Suppose he has had to go away or has already gone to the office? But a familiar voice answered the ringing and she started at once with, 'The car has broken down.'

'Broken down! Do you mean you have had an accident?

Where are you?'

'No, no, the brakes have given way,' replied Janet. 'I am here in the village near my old home. I had to walk, the car is not safe to drive, what shall I do? Can you come and fetch me?'

'Steady on,' replied Will. 'What do you mean, come and fetch you? I have something to tell you, I have had bad news since you left and my wife is coming back to live with me, it's all a mistake, you don't want all the trauma of a divorce case and neither do I. Everything is settled here and all you have to do is to make it up with your husband. You can have the car for a present, you can soon get the brakes fixed, it's a good little car, you will be a lot happier with your husband who loves you and your old familiar life.'

Janet was too horrified to answer, she stared at the mouthpiece of the telephone, she had reversed the charges, and just stood there trying to gather her thoughts. 'All for nothing,' kept ringing through her brain. 'What shall I do, what shall I do?'

'Are you still there?' came the voice.

'Yes, I am still here, I don't know what to say, I thought you loved me.'

'Of course I love you,' replied Will, 'but you must see that what we planned is not practical, already I have laid out a lot of money. There is too much difference in our ages, we can never be happy together, my wife is used to me and can look after me. I am a busy man and need an understanding wife. I will pack up your things and send them back to you. Tell me again your address, I don't think I ever had it.'

Janet started to give the familiar address of the cottage, asking herself how long she would be able to call it home. As if in a dream she replaced the receiver and left the phone box, starting to walk back to the cottage. 'What shall I do, what shall I do?' kept repeating itself in her brain, she had completely forgotten the car and the attention it needed.

7

Walking slowly, it took Janet a long time to reach the familiar muddy road and to arrive at the cottage. The door was open and standing inside was Mrs Cannon, the wife of her husband's employer. 'Where is Sam?' she asked, evincing no surprise at seeing Janet there.

'I don't know,' replied Janet. 'I have just come home and as he was not here I went to the village to telephone a friend. My car brakes have given out.'

Mrs Cannon did not seem surprised to see Janet there but again remarked that it seemed strange that Sam had not made his usual morning call at the farmhouse, and said that he was in the middle of ploughing up the field by the river but neither Sam nor the tractor was to be seen in the field. Janet did not know what to say and thankfully collapsed into a chair.

'What time did you arrive?' asked Mrs Cannon. 'Thought you were away.'

'Yes, I have been away in Scotland with friends for a time and have only just arrived back. As the car brakes were faulty and I didn't want to wake Sam up too early, I have travelled through the night, and decided to go and telephone first.'

'I see,' said Mrs Cannon. 'Well, I don't know what to do, I suppose Sam will turn up with the tractor in due course, he always knows best what to do.' She went off towards the farmhouse.

Janet sat down and tried to recover her sanity. 'What has happened to me? Now I have no one and no income, I suppose I can sell the car but I shall have to get the brakes repaired first. I shall have to get a job. What kind of job, I wonder? It's no use my calling on Father, he said I had made my bed and must lie on it.'

She busied herself in the cottage, there was lots to do, the bed to change and sheets to wash. She went to the pump and filled a pail to put into the old copper in the corner of the kitchen. I must chop some more wood and get in some logs, she thought, or the fire will go out again. All the old unpleasant routine came back to her with sickening familiarity. The house was lonely and seemed weird without Sam. The dog seemed restless and kept looking as if he were listening. For a footstep I suppose, thought Janet. One that he will never hear again, and she broke down in tears. All that had happened seemed so unreal to her, surely, she thought, I shall wake up soon and find it all has been a terrible dream. Oh, to see Sam walk in that door again! Then a picture of his white face with the gash and the blood all streaming down over one eye and the matted hair seemed to appear and she shuddered. Am I going to be haunted for ever now, what can I do? I shall go mad. She looked into a corner cupboard and found a bottle of aspirins. For a few moments as she held the bottle in her hand she felt tempted to swallow the lot. I don't suppose there are enough in the bottle to finish me off, she thought, and took two before she rested, hoping that the terrible headache would ease.

She must have slept for a long time. Suddenly she was aware of knocking. She went to the door and found Mr and Mrs Cannon there.

'We are afraid that we have some very bad news for you, my dear,' Mrs Cannon started. 'Sam must have had an accident with the tractor early this morning, it must have got out of control and ran down the bank into the river, it is very deep just there you know. There has been a lot of rain lately, the bank is muddy and the river is very much deeper than usual, some men are now dragging the tractor out.'

'Poor Sam must have started work very early this morning before you got here,' said Mr Cannon.

Mrs Cannon looked pityingly at the stricken girl. 'Try not to fret dear,' she said, 'We will look after you for a bit, you can come to the house with us if you like until we see what the arrangements are.'

'I think I would rather stay here,' Janet said. She wanted to be alone to gather her thoughts in the light of the new turn of events. She still seemed to be in a dream world.

Mr and Mrs Cannon left after reassuring Janet that they were her friends and would help her through the difficult time ahead.

The next few days were almost like a nightmare to the girl, she passed the time as if in a dream and finally when Mrs Cannon came to tell her that an inquest had been fixed and that Janet was welcome to stay in the cottage as long as she wished, she felt as if she could sleep and sleep and never wake up. The dog, however, was the best friend she seemed to have and he finally saved her reason, she afterwards thought. He stayed beside her as if he knew that she needed him and, of course, he needed food which reminded her that she too must eat. In due course the local baker arrived and brought the usual parcel of necessities which Janet was thankful to have in spite of the fact that it took most of her money to pay for them. The baker had heard the news and was very sympathetic, he said never mind about the bill until all was settled but Janet had no idea what was to be settled or what she had to do. She relied completely on Mrs Cannon who seemed to take the matter in hand. She took the girl to the inquest, arranged the funeral and said that there was a sum of money due to Janet through an insurance.

Accidental death was the verdict and after the funeral Janet was at last able to collect her thoughts enough to agree to look for a post for herself. Mrs Cannon brought several likely looking advertisements to her notice and she wrote to apply for each.

'Please, someone, love me, please, please, oh what shall I do? I have no one. No one to love and care for, no one to love me.' Each night as she lay tossing, waiting for sleep she called aloud. The dog licked her hand. 'At least he loves me,' Janet thought.

Days passed and it seemed as if no one wanted Janet's services. Mrs Cannon called and offered her a job at the farmhouse. 'You could take on the cleaning you know, and there are milk pans in the dairy to be scoured every day. I could find you lots to do and you could stay in the cottage for a time. Of course we shall want it for another man in due course.'

'Thank you,' said Janet, 'but I would rather go right away if possible.' She hoped that it would not be necessary to work in the house where her one time schoolfriend often came to stay. She must try to get some kind of work where she could live in the house. She went to the village library and was aimlessly looking at magazines when an advertisement caught her eye. A widowed farmer was seeking a lady to look after his house.

The milk went away and the farm was in a pleasant part of Shropshire. Amongst the posts vacant that she saw this one seemed the most promising somehow. She had made a call on the village garage and they had promised to attend to her car. She went back to the cottage and wrote out an application for the post.

Sooner than she expected Janet received a reply from the farmer fixing a date and an easily accessible meeting place. The day soon arrived and the car was also now in good order and she set out hopefully to meet the farmer.

He turned out to be quite homely looking and dressed cleanly but rather roughly. He said that he had a teenage son who was at home helping on the farm. His wife had died a year ago and he missed her very much. After a chat and a cup of tea, Janet told him of her husband's accident, that a tractor that he was driving went out of control and plunged down a steep bank into a river. The farmer said that he would be pleased to start as soon as she liked. Janet replied that she had only to clear out her cottage and could perhaps come to some arrangement with Mrs Cannon about the furniture, what there was of it, which was not worth very much. She was anxious to keep her car, she said, as she had only just learnt to drive and did not want to get out of practice. 'Don't worry about that,' said Mr Greaves. 'I shall be pleased for you to drive the family car any time you wish to, there will be plenty of opportunity.'

Janet went back to the cottage feeling quite pleased that she had secured a post and somewhere to live quite quickly. She talked things over with Mrs Cannon who offered to purchase the furniture and said that they would have a better chance of finding an occupier for the cottage if it was furnished. Janet felt very sad at leaving the only home she had. Although it was poor, she had come to it full of hope and plans for the future with Sam, the first real home she had acquired of her own. She accepted the first offer she had for the car, the garage owner said he would be glad to take it, and Janet had no idea of its value but was pleased to have some real money of her own at last.

8

Janet's first day at Greaves Farm was passed trying to acquaint herself with all that she found there and to arrange some agreement about what her duties would actually be. 'I am quite easy to please,' said Mr Greaves. 'I would be glad if we could use Christian names, mine is Arthur and my son in Arthur too, so we call him Art. We do enjoy a hearty breakfast but it is usually about eight thirty when we come into the house after early milking. The milk is collected and the empty churns are left here for afternoon milking. I would like the churns washed out as, although they are supposed to be clean when they arrive I prefer to give them another clean out. I will show you later what there is to do in the dairy. My late wife used to set some milk in a large pan each day and skim off the cream to make some butter for the house. It was a fad of hers, she made cream cheese also but we have not had any of that either since she died. It is up to you to make your own plans about that and other things. Regarding the poultry, they have been a bit neglected lately, we have been so busy dipping the sheep, and of course sowing the seeds, but my wife used to look after them and often had quite a few eggs to sell. It was her little hobby and she used to save the money, together with what she made sometimes from selling old hens for boiling that she had no use for.'

Janet found the days went quickly. She was kept very busy and was rather surprised to find that there were no signs of neglect anywhere in the house. The two men had a bedroom each at the rear of the farmhouse and hers was at the front and looked out over a view of gently rolling hills and valleys with winding roads and sheep grazing. I think I could be happy here, she thought. There does not seem too much to do and at least it won't be so lonely as the old cottage was. Her mind was beginning to wake up again after the torpor that had taken possession of her brain after the accident with her husband. Arthur did not allude to him in any way after the first explanation of his accident and Janet was grateful. She was trying to forget all that had happened over the past weeks, in fact she tried to empty her mind and to resume life again if possible with the outlook of a single girl.

Market day came and she enjoyed a visit to the town and a shopping round, looking for a few bargains in underwear and a dress. It was a long time since she had enjoyed having money in her pocket, money of her own to spend as she liked. Mrs Cannon had been quite generous over the furniture and Janet was relieved to have the whole affair settled. There was also some insurance money to come as there had been a farm insurance against accidents. Janet did not try to understand anything about this and was glad to leave it to the Cannons to settle it for her. They in their turn were glad that Janet had found for herself a steady job.

Janet soon found that young Art, although a very shy young man, was very helpful and welcomed any opportunity to talk to her and offered to supply her with a gun if she would care to try some pigeon shooting. There were lots of birds, he explained, that were a pest on the farm, there were also of course useful birds and they tried to keep the pests down by shooting as many as possible. One day when they were walking over the fields together, Art asked her if his father had said anything at all to her that might be upsetting.

'How do you mean?' asked Janet.

'Well, I don't know if I should tell you this, but you seem like a nice girl and I would not like you to be upset or offended.'

'In what way?' asked Janet, feeling intrigued.

Art looked very embarrassed and said, 'I can't say, but lock your bedroom door at night.'

Janet was astounded at this remark and stopped, staring at Art, whose face had developed a deep flush.

'I can't say any more, I wish I had not said that,' he stammered out.

They walked on in silence. Janet began to think. Arthur certainly had started a habit of walking upstairs sometimes when she was brushing her hair or getting ready to go out and had stood in her bedroom doorway making her feel rather uncomfortable, but she had taken no notice of that. It didn't seem to be important. Now she began to think. Yes, he had seemed to stand about rather and to watch her when she was busy, when he could have been reading the paper or looking at television in the evening. But as the days passed she forgot the subject and continued to leave her bedroom door open when she was making the bed or tidying the room as she did with all the other rooms in the house.

One night she had retired rather early, feeling tired, and had taken a sleeping pill to try to sleep off a headache. Suddenly she was startled into wakefulness feeling a hand drawing back her hair from around her face. It was dark and very little light penetrated through the side of the drawn curtains over the window. 'Hush,' a voice said, 'Don't shout, I won't hurt you.' She recognized Arthur's voice.

'What do you want,' she whispered.

'A little kindness,' Arthur replied. 'I am a lonely man and it would not hurt you to be kind to me, don't make a sound, we don't want to wake Art up, do we?'

'Go away,' said Janet. 'If you don't I shall scream.'

'Oh no you won't,' said Arthur and pressed his hand over her mouth. Janet opened her teeth and sunk them into a finger, Arthur gasped with pain and took his hand away at once. 'All right my girl. Have it your own way, but I could have made life very happy for you here you know, now you have spoilt it,' and he turned away and left the bedroom. Janet got very little more sleep that night as she recalled the hint of warning that Art had given her.

She tried to decide next morning as she dressed if she should tell Art what had happened. She cooked the usual breakfast and, leaving it in the oven of the large range with the door slightly open, she busied herself in the dairy feeling unable to face Arthur over the breakfast table.

I suppose I shall have to look for another job now, she told herself. How unlucky can I be? I am lonely, the men I have met that I could love and respect are not interested in me. The others, those I cannot bear to be near, seem to get interested in me and want to become familiar.

As the day passed things seemed much as usual. There was always plenty to do on the farm and in the house and the family usually only met at mealtimes and for an hour in the evening.

Janet decided that on her next visit to town she would try to buy a magazine or newspaper of some kind that might advertise another suitable post where she could live in and try again. There seemed to be nothing suitable for some time and she thought she would have to put up with things until she could get somewhere else to go. Arthur seemed sullen and quiet and took very little notice of her. He did not offer her the car to go to town at all and she waited for a bus which passed the end of the lane and went into town.

One day when she had almost given up looking she found an advertisement for a lady to drive a car and to be a companion to a widowed lady. She hastened to write a letter of application and to address it to the box number given. She went back to the farm feeling more hopeful and happier than she had felt for a long time. A driving job! She could scarcely believe her luck. Oh, if only she could get this job! Days went by and then weeks, soon her first month at the farm would have passed. She wondered if she would have to give a month's notice to leave. She had almost given up any hope of a reply when one morning the postman brought her a letter. It was a reply to her application for the post. Mrs Kinder would be glad to see her if she could call at the address given on Tuesday at three pm, or write or telephone to arrange another appointment. Janet could scarcely believe her luck. In her mind she had already obtained the post and could not stop herself confiding in Art who said that he was really sorry that she had to leave them but could understand why and felt very ashamed of his father. 'He is lonely you know,' was all he could think of to say. 'It has been lovely having you here, it has cheered me up a lot.'

'I haven't got the job yet,' said Janet. 'But I do hope I am successful.' She had difficulty in controlling her desire to go about the house singing. She answered the letter and accepted the appointment and at length the day came. She had little difficulty in finding the house which was in the city suburbs and looked very imposing. She had managed to get Arthur's rather surly consent to borrow the car saying that she had some calls to make in the town.

* * *

Entering the side gate into the short drive she left the old car outside and walked up the door and rang the bell. A young, rather pert looking maid answered and ushered her into a well-furnished room where there sat an elderly but active looking lady. 'That will do Winnie,' she said and, 'Come and sit here' to Janet. Her sharp and beady eyes travelled over the girl's clothes and shoes then settled penetratingly on the face. 'You say that you can drive a car?'

'Yes, I passed my driving test in Scotland.'

'Oh, that's a good thing. I have heard that the Scots are very particular about that kind of thing. When could you start, Miss?'

'Janet Ellis.'

She was rather surprised to hear herself referred to as Miss, but decided on the spot not to contradict the lady.

'I think I could start almost at once. What would my salary be?'

'We should not fall out about that if you gave satisfaction, I will tell you what your duties would be, it is a very easy job really, you saw my maid Winnie, she does all the housework and the cooking. You might be asked to lay the table or see to the flowers, and perhaps to take my son's breakfast up to his room occasionally. He does not have very good health and he is slightly crippled. He is very sensitive about it. He does really need some help but won't admit it. He is not allowed to drive the car and I never learnt to drive. It would be your main job to look after the car, I will show it to you directly, and to deliver my son wherever he wants to go, mostly to his club. At present he is forced to take a taxi and goes every day after breakfast and stays there most days for lunch. You will collect him after lunch and bring him home, then take him back to the club about seven pm where he will have dinner. He usually has a taxi home anyway as he is very late in the evening. So you can see that it is a very easy job. Both my son and I have breakfast upstairs, we rise very late. Winnie sees to that and prepares lunch. You might help by laying the table for lunch occasionally. You will have lunch and tea with me, do you understand? Do you drink, Miss Ellis?'

'I drink very little, perhaps a small sherry before lunch,' replied Janet.

'Are you satisfied with the job? Both you and Winnie will be very satisfied if you have any sense, you wouldn't get another job like this easily.'

'Yes, I think I would like to take the job,' said Janet, 'as long as the salary is satisfactory.'

'What are you having now?' was the next question and Janet named the figure honestly.

'I will start you at the same and increase it after a month if you are satisfactory,' was the reply. 'When can you start?'

'As soon as you like.'

Janet thankfully arranged a satisfactory date. She was not very worried about being able to leave the farm and was sure that Arthur's guilty conscience would stop any argument. The only regret she had in leaving was Art, he had been genuinely fond of her and, longing for love and affection, Janet's lonely heart had taken some kind of solace from his kindness. Perhaps he would remain friends and might call to see her sometimes.

As Janet said goodbye and left the house she went to look in the garage to see what kind of car was there. Winnie the maid was hovering in the background and could no longer restrain her curiosity. She followed Janet into the garage.

'Would you like a cup of tea?' she asked.

'Oh yes,' replied Janet.

'Come along then,' Winnie led the way along the back of the house to the kitchen.

'Who does the garden?' asked Janet.

'Oh, a man comes regularly to cut the grass and he grows some vegetables for us too, are you going to take the job then? You are the best one she's seen I think, she is a queer old bird but I can manage her, she couldn't do without me you see, do you know what you will have to do?'

'Oh yes, drive the car mostly, to take her son to a club and fetch him back, is that all he does?'

Winnie laughed. 'You'll find out,' she said. 'It's not my place to tell you what you have to do, I get on all right with them and they are not short of money. He was in the navy until he got something come in his legs. He's got a job to walk but he's worse at night, that's why he has a taxi home, the taxi man puts him to bed.' Winnie gave a penetrating look to see Janet's reaction to this piece of knowledge.

'We should not be talking about them like this you know,' said Janet. 'Mrs Kinder might come into the kitchen.'

'There's no fear of that, she always goes to sleep after lunch until tea time.'

'What time does she get up?'

Winnie shot a sharp look across the kitchen table. 'She gets up late, just in time to see me laying the table for lunch, then, after lunch she goes to lie down until tea time.'

'What does she do after tea?'

'Oh, she stays up very late, I don't know what time she goes to bed but she always waits up until the Captain is brought home, she sees that he is safely in bed. Sometimes, but not very often, they stay up, drinking together after he gets back from the club. I know because she always put the empty bottles in the dustbin before she goes to bed, but mind you, I always make sure that I am well out of the way when she's about at night, she gets in a foul temper, she will go out into the kitchen and examine all the pans to see if they are clean and will look into the fridge to see that I am not wasting anything. I have learnt my lesson over that, I never take any notice of her when she is in one of her moods. If she gets too bad I give in my notice. That brings her to her senses, she knows she can't do without me.'

Janet was amazed to hear this diatribe and hastened to stop the girl. 'We should not be talking like this,' she said, 'I must go now but I hope and expect to be here to stay very soon, perhaps tomorrow.'

'All right Miss, I am sure we shall get on fine.'

Janet hurried away and soon arrived back at the farm with her news. Arthur was taking a short after-lunch nap.

'What's all this then? I thought you were never coming back you were so long.'

'I want to leave, at once if you please, my month's trial is up in two days, I have got another job.'

'Oh, have you? Leaving us in the lurch are you? After all I have done for you, let you have the car to use as you like, what about my son, how is he going to manage?'

'I only came on a month's trial remember.'

Arthur stood over her threateningly and Janet began to feel afraid. 'You don't care a rap about us, you selfish cat.'

'There's no need to get nasty, I could report you to the police you know.'

'Don't be ridiculous, I should only have to say you asked for it, trying to get into my bed.'

At this remark Janet began to feel more afraid. 'Give me my wages and I will leave at once.'

'Not likely, you are leaving without a month's notice and I am entitled to stop a month's wages for that so I owe you nothing.'

Janet felt very angry at this remark but did not know if he was right. She hated the thought of any fuss and only wanted to get away from him for ever. She had spent more money lately than she had intended or really could afford. She did not like the idea of working another month at the farm and also felt sure that Mrs Kinder would not be prepared to keep the driving job open for that length of time.

'Come now,' she said, 'surely we can part friends, I shall not be far away, I can perhaps come over to see you sometimes.'

Arthur looked surprised to hear this remark and a crafty look came over his surly face. 'Oh, I thought you didn't like me, perhaps I was jumping the gun a bit, I like you, you know, you are a nice looking gel and I am looking for a wife. You wouldn't be doing too bad for yourself if you came here you know, and Art likes you.'

'You wouldn't be asking me to marry you?'

'That's about the size of it.'

Words trembled on Janet's tongue. She started to say 'I wouldn't marry you if you were the last man on earth', but discretion came to her rescue and she said, 'You never know, our friendship might develop if given a chance, now I must get on and collect my things.' Janet went towards the staircase followed by Arthur who looked rather dejected.

'I will give you a cheque, will that do?'

'Yes of course, say goodbye to Art for me will you?'

'Yes of course, but you must let us have your address.'

'Here it is, I have written it down.' Janet thankfully escaped and packing her meagre collection of clothes hurried from the house.

Catching a bus Janet had little trouble in getting to The Limes and Mrs Kinder was pleased to see her. 'Will you like to have a look at the car and get used to it? You could get the tank filled and see if anything else is wanted, we have not used it for some time, I hope you know how to look after a car, I don't trust the young man at the garage.'

'Oh yes,' replied Janet hastily. 'If you get on all right here I expect you will be able to use the car sometimes for yourself if you need it, do you like lobster?'

'What a strange question to fire at anyone, I don't know, I have never had any.'

Gathering up the car keys Janet went to start the car. The car was much larger than the small one she had been used to and even larger and more up-to-date than the farmer's car, but quite like the one she had used when learning to drive. It seemed to start quite easily and soon she was at the garage. A nice looking young man came out and asked, 'Are you the new young lady at Mrs Kinder's place? I recognize the car.'

Janet thought he seemed a very nice looking fellow and so polite. 'Yes, I expect I shall see quite a lot of you, I have to collect her son every day.'

'What, that old soak? Oh, sorry, I didn't mean to say that, it's none of my business anyway.'

'Just fill the car up, look at the oil and check the tyres please.'

'There you are then. My name is Jack, shall I put it on the account?'

'Yes please, I shall be seeing you I expect.'

'Yes, what is your name Miss? I can tell you are a stranger around her, do you come from Scotland?'

Janet was not aware that she had picked up an accent during the short time that she had been in the north, she had admired the way Will had talked and others, now she realized that she had deliberately tried to imitate them and to cultivate their accent.

'I am Welsh anyway, and you can call on me if you get into difficulties any time.'

'Thank you, it is nice to know someone in a strange place,' replied Janet as she drove away.

Back at The Limes Winnie was laying the table for the evening meal. 'The mistress told me to lay a place for you,' she said. 'I hope you like lobster, I can't stand it myself, I don't know why she gets it, nearly all shell, I call it.'

'What time is dinner?'

'Seven o'clock.'

Winnie hurried back to the kitchen.

Janet found her hostess very well-dressed and waiting in the dining-room when she came down at seven o'clock. 'Will you have a glass of sherry?' she asked. 'I usually have a half-bottle of white wine with dinner but I know that not everyone likes that.'

Janet replied that she seldom took much to drink but would enjoy the sherry and would also like a small glass of white wine if it was sweet.

'Tell me a bit about yourself,' asked Mrs Kinder.

They sat enjoying coffee after an excellent meal.

'There's not much to tell, my mother died when I was young and my father married again. They are not very interested in me, I had to look for some way of earning a living.'

'I am sorry to hear that,' replied Mrs Kinder. 'I lost my husband a long time ago and my son suffers with his legs. He is a good son really but the pain makes him a bit bad tempered sometimes, you must not take any notice of that, if he takes to you he will probably be very happy for the companionship of a nice girl. He is very lonely, I wish he did not spend so much time at his club, it is a long time since he stayed at home to have a meal with me, if we had pleasant company like yourself I feel sure he would stay at home for dinner. You won't be able to meet him until tomorrow, he will be ready about eleven o'clock for you to drive him to his club, he will stay there for lunch and you can have yours with me, then take the car to fetch him home about two thirty, he will go again about six thirty when he has had his afternoon sleep. He has to take this every day, doctor's orders. You can take him but he won't be ready to come home until very late and he has arranged for his usual man to bring him home.'

Janet was beginning to feel curious about the Captain, as he was called. She retired early and in spite of having a nice bedroom and a very comfortable bed she did not seem to be able to get to sleep. Several times she heard voices and noises and came to the conclusion that the people in this house were very much more awake during the night than they were during the day. She lay awake suffering her usual longing to be a part of someone's life, to be loved. Loved by someone that she could love and admire in return, not just a man who wanted a companion to sleep with and to cook for him. A real man. One that she could respect but one that really loved her, the longing for love grew and grew. Sometimes she had difficulty in overcoming the urge to end her useless seeming life. How could she endure a lonely existence? She had so much love of offer. Would she never have the chance to lavish it on anyone who would return it in a true and genuine way? Sam had loved her in his fashion. It had been comforting when they first met to find that she was attractive to someone, but his love savoured of animals and farm life. It was too crude for words and often offended her finer feelings. The love that Will had offered was refined and gentle. What had she done to lose that for good? She had deceived him of course. She must never try to build her happiness on deceit again, if the chance ever came. It seemed fairly obvious that Mrs Kinder had vague hopes of getting her son to show interest. Janet was getting very curious about the man and finally she fell asleep wondering what the new day would bring.

Next morning Janet got up at eight o'clock having been awake listening for a long time hearing no sound. She dressed and went downstairs, entering the kitchen from where she seemed to detect some sign of life. She came upon Winnie who looked startled. Winnie had a cup of tea on the table and a poached egg on a plate, she was obviously enjoying her breakfast and jumped up quickly to fetch another cup and saucer. Pouring out the tea she asked Janet what she would like for breakfast and if she would mind having it in the kitchen to save work.

'Of course not,' said Janet. 'If you tell me where things are I will get it myself,' and she proceeded to get plates and to cut some bread. The two sat together eating and talking.

Winnie was very young, it appeared, and she told Janet she had only recently left school and that she was one of a very large family. Her mother was glad to get her 'legs under someone else's table', she said. Janet could see that the girl was glad to have someone to talk to and sat listening whilst she rambled on.

'The mistress doesn't have breakfast, she is up very late at night helping the Captain to bed and she likes to be left alone in the morning. I am glad she does not come down until lunch time because she is so bad tempered in the morning, you would not recognize her before lunch.' The girl looked sideways at Janet to see how this information was being received and meeting only friendly eyes and a smile she continued, 'I shall take an omelette up to the Captain about half past nine, he will have it in bed and then he will get dressed and ready to go to his club. You wouldn't like the mistress in the morning, I always hope that she will not come down until lunch time. She is so bad tempered, she finds fault with everything. I tell her off sometimes, then she gives me notice to leave. I don't take any notice of her as I know she will forget all about it afterwards. She pokes her nose into everything. She asks what knife I use to prepare the vegetables and how long it is since I washed out the dusters. I put up with it for a bit but if it gets too bad I give in my notice, that soon shuts her up.'

'You shouldn't talk about Mrs Kinder like that,' said Janet horrified.

'Oh good gracious, she wouldn't mind, we understand each other. She would be lost without me you know, she drinks,' and Winnie leaned over and whispered the last few words as if in confidence. 'I know better than to go up to her room in the morning. I did go once, wondering why she was so quiet. I thought that something had happened to her and as I knocked and could get no reply I opened the door and went in. She lay there fast asleep with her mouth wide open and two bottles on the floor, empty. She always brings empty bottles down in a basket under some clothes and puts them in the dustbin, covering them over with newspapers, but I know they are there. She can't help it you know, and the Captain is the same, he is brought home half asleep every night and carried upstairs and put to bed. I suppose I should not have told you all this but you would have found it out sooner or later. You must not be too bothered about it, they can't help it you know, they are nice people really. You need not get up too early, I will bring you a cup of tea up tomorrow and you can get up slowly. There is never anyone about until almost lunch time, you could lay the table then.'

'All right,' said Janet, 'but I have to take the Captain to his club at eleven o'clock.'

'Oh, I see, they have sacked the chap with the taxi then.'

'He will bring him home at night I believe,' Janet replied.

'I see,' said Winnie, 'I must get on with my work now, I tell you what you could do if you like, arrange some flowers in the vases.'

'All right, I will do that and then I must get the car ready to take the Captain to his club at eleven o'clock.'

She busied herself walking around the garden in search of flowers for the house. At eleven o'clock Janet had got the car ready and brought it up to the side door. The hall was quite capacious and as she stood waiting for the Captain to appear she could scarcely contain her curiosity. Then she heard him come to the top of the stairs and start to descend. He was tall, and what she had heard described as a well-built figure, a little overweight. Obviously he had some difficulty in controlling the movement of his legs as he descended the stairs but Janet waited until he got to the foot, turned round and spoke to her.

'You must be Janet,' he said. 'How are you?' and put out his hand. 'I suppose you have got the car outside, I used to drive you know, but my legs are not reliable now. Do you like driving?'

'Yes, I was very pleased to pass my test.'

'Yes of course, I forgot about that, I shall enjoy being driven by you I know, Mother tells me you are single and looking for a husband.'

Janet was astounded by these remarks and started to feel very angry but the Captain gave a hearty laugh and said, 'Of course I am joking, my mother would never say anything remotely like that and I have never been married and I am sure no girl would have me these days anyway.'

Janet felt obliged to reply and said that she was sure the Captain would find the right girl one day. Soon, taking instructions from the Captain, Janet arrived at the club and drew up outside the door. A uniformed man appeared, he had obviously been waiting for the Captain to arrive. He came forward and helped him into the club. He seemed pleased to see a woman driver and asked if she would be collecting the Captain later. 'Yes,' replied Janet, 'and I shall see you every day if all goes well.'

Lunch was a protracted meal and afterwards Janet asked if she could play the piano, 'That is if you don't mind.'

'Of course not, I shall be very glad, the piano should be played more, I am so glad you play. An old friend of mine will be coming to stay soon, she has been in musical comedy and is getting too old now but she will love to hear the piano played, I am sure. You will see that it is a very old one and I am afraid that I have not kept it tuned but now we can get a tuner to come. It will be worth while. You will like my friend I think, she is quite elderly now of course but she looks young still.'

Janet amused herself playing by ear but the instrument was so much out of tune that it did not sound anything like the music she knew and loved. *Traumerei*, *Salut D'Amour* and others were so unrecognizable that she gave up in despair. The days seemed to pass slowly and uneventfully and Janet was pleased when the day came to go and meet the musical comedy artist at the railway station. Janet speculated in her mind what kind of lady it would turn out to be. No picture she could have formed in her wildest dreams would have been anything like the woman who came waddling out of the station entrance. Short, fat, a lined wizened face topped a grotesque warped body. Her face was a dirty brown but strangest of all was her hair which shone out like a copper coloured tangle of curls. Behind her came a disgruntled looking official carrying a large and very shabby looking suitcase covered with gay labels naming countries all over the world. Janet was so busy studying this vision that she did not realize that they were coming straight towards the car. The woman directed the porter to place the cases inside and Janet suddenly realized that this must be the Madame Susette she had come to meet and jumped out of the car at once. Madame said she had recognized the car and seemed very pleased to see Janet. 'You are just as I expected,' she said, 'and I am so glad that my dear friend Alice has found you. What do you think of the Captain?'

Janet was rather taken aback by such a direct question, she had heard about the easy manners and friendliness of people on the stage and could now understand how this idea had developed.

Soon they arrived at the house and Mrs Kinder came forward to welcome her friend. Janet put the car away and came to join the two later over a cup of tea. On closer acquaintance Madame did not seem quite so unusual and Janet soon left the two together. She made the usual journey with the Captain who had entered the lounge for a few moments to speak to Madame and to ask her how she was, and called at the garage to refill the petrol tank. Jack came out looking very pleased to see her and to her surprise he asked if she liked dancing.

'What kind of dancing?' asked Janet. 'Do you mean ballet?'

'No, just dancing, I think they call it old-fashioned dancing now, and sequence dancing. I belong to a club, we meet once a week, I like the waltz, foxtrot, tango and all the old ones. I wondered if you would like to come with me on Thursday?'

'Where is it held?' asked Janet.

'At the hall just down the road, you must have seen it, we meet at seven o'clock and usually finish about ten thirty. I am sure you would have a good time if you like dancing.'

'I am not too sure about that,' said Janet. She had been to dances occasionally with her husband in the past and had quite enjoyed herself, but recently she had formed the opinion that modern dancing was much too noisy and not for her. 'Can I let you know?' she asked.

'All right but don't wait too long, I have to get a partner or it's no use going.'

'As far as I know I can go,' replied Janet. 'But who did you take before?'

'The girl I used to go with has moved away.'

'All right, I will meet you here at about seven fifteen on Thursday then. What kind of clothes do they wear?'

'Anything will do as long as it's comfortable, especially shoes, they must be comfortable, oh, you know what I mean, I will look forward to seeing you on Thursday then.'

'All right,' said Janet, and drove away.

9

Next morning Janet came down to the kitchen as usual to find Winnie preparing a tray for the new guest. 'She likes fruit juice, cereal and a lightly boiled egg with a pot of tea, bread and butter and marmalade,' she announced. 'Would you like to take it up to her?'

'I don't mind,' replied Janet and started off with the tray. She knocked on the bedroom door and heard a muffled 'Come in'. Entering the room was difficult, it was so dark but she managed to find her way to the window and draw back the heavy curtains. Turning around towards the bed she was completely taken aback. The head of brilliant copper curls reposed on a bedpost at the foot of the bed. It took Janet some time to collect her wits, there had been no accident. The lady in the bed was not headless, only hairless. Janet felt very embarrassed and tried not to look at the lined face surrounded by a frill of lace, tied under the chin, that reposed on the pillow.

'Don't be surprised my dear, you must have seen a wig before, wait until you get to my age, you will probably have to wear one yourself by then.'

Janet had some difficulty in acting naturally as she recovered from the shock, she placed the tray on the bedside table and turned to help the queer looking lady to sit up in the bed.

'Sit down for a moment my dear, I want to talk to you, do you like it here?'

'Yes, I think so, I have scarcely been here long enough to tell yet.'

'Yes, I realize that, but you know what my friend Alice is planning to do?'

'No, I am afraid I know very little of Mrs Kinder's plans.'

'She wants to find a wife for the Captain, her son, you know.'

'Oh does she?' Janet could scarcely hide her surprise and anger at this information, as far as she knew the Captain had taken very little notice of her up to the present, he was polite but only just so, no conversation had passed between them at all. 'Does the Captain know about this?' she asked.

'I don't know about that of course but my friend Alice, whom I have known for a very long time has asked me if I would see what you have to say about the suggestion, she is very shy with strangers you know and doesn't like meeting people.'

'Well, you can tell her that I have no wish to marry at present and if I did I would not expect other people to arrange it for me.'

'You mustn't be offended my dear, Alice likes you very much and would welcome you as a daughter-in-law. You could be very well taken care of here, both financially and otherwise.'

'They want to buy me, you mean?' said Janet angrily.

'Don't put it like that my dear, we will say no more about it at present but I understand that you have no relatives.'

'I have a father,' said Janet, 'but I don't want to hear any more about the subject,' and she left the room looking back at the strange head with its frill around it who had now picked up teeth from a side table cup and was now putting them to good use. Janet felt quite sick as she returned to the kitchen. Winnie looked laughingly at her, 'Got a shock did you?' she asked. 'I did the first time I saw her in bed, but she's not a bad old dear, she always gives me a present when she leaves and she's not hard to please, you will get used to her.' I hope not, thought Janet.

The morning passed slowly, Janet took the Captain to his club and in the light of the new information she had recently gathered she took a sideways look at his face and watched him as he walked into the club. He seemed to have difficulty in walking but otherwise looked quite upright and almost military in his bearing, quite different to Arthur, she thought, who was somewhat bent and worn looking with a very ruddy face. The Captain looked pale and had a rather harassed expression almost always, but Janet had got used to that and the thought occurred to her that being married to him could not be very different to being chauffeur and erstwhile companion to his mother. Janet felt more and more the need for someone to love, and one who would return that love. She knew that she had some kind of attraction for the opposite sex but could not understand where the attraction lay. She knew that she had very dark brown eyes and was quite well blessed with the usual attributes that women seem to desire, she knew that she had a friendly nature and was always willing to help others, perhaps that was the secret. The kind of people that so far she had found did not seem to return the love and affection she had lavished on them.

After dinner that evening the two ladies invited her to sit and talk. Mrs Kinder as usual had little to say and tarried for a long time over her dinner but tonight she seemed anxious to get the meal over and Madame Susette said, 'Why don't you take Janet — I may call you Janet? — up to the attic and show her the things you have stored, Alice?'

'All right, come along then,' said Mrs Kinder and led the way upstairs and up another flight to the attic, a very large room under the roof. A series of large trunks stood about and Mrs Kinder took out a key and unlocked one of the largest. 'This one is full of family heirlooms, silver we do not use, I don't care to trust it to the tender mercies of Winnie. It will belong to my son one day of course, and his children.'

'I did not know he had any children,' said Janet, surprised at the remark.

'My son wants children and so do I of course, a grandson would be a great joy to me, we have no other family.'

'Was your son wounded in the war?' asked Janet.

'Oh no, he had rheumatic fever as a child, quite badly, he was lucky to be no worse. He copes very well, he is rather shy you know, and seems to retire more and more into his shell.'

Janet did not know what to reply to this, she looked at the ugly, heavy looking silver and wondered how anyone could possibly treasure such horrid looking articles. I suppose they are very valuable, she thought.

'I am hoping to get him away from that club, it is the only place he goes to and I am sure he would be much happier and a great deal better off if he gave up going there every day.'

Then the old lady seemed suddenly to remember what she had brought Janet up to the attic for. 'Now come along and see what I have here,' she said, walking over to another large trunk. This one was not locked and she lifted the heavy lid to disclose thick layers of tissue paper, removing this she then lifted out, one by one, a series of beautiful, luxurious looking dresses, both day and evening wear, also a large parcel of beautiful underwear. A mink coat, several short fur coats and various oddments. 'What do you think of these?' she asked. 'Of course the fur coats have to go into cold storage throughout the summer but I can't resist having them where I can at least see them through the rest of the year.'

'How lovely,' said Janet enraptured. 'Where did they come from? They look quite new.'

'Yes, they have been kept well and many of the styles have come back into fashion again now I notice. They were all mine when I first married. My husband seemed as if he could not buy me enough. I loved him very much and when he died I had no heart to wear nice clothes. They would fit you, I think, and they are all yours. You do realize, of course, that I have plans for you to interest my son in yourself, so that he will think about marriage and I hope propose to you.'

Janet did not know what to reply to this, she looked at the clothes and thought, 'If only I had just one of those dresses, or a real fur coat, I would be so happy. Why does the old lady think she can bribe me, I wonder?'

She turned away and said, 'Shall we go down now?' She helped to close the trunk. 'Madame will be missing you.'

Mrs Kinder turned to go. 'Do you think you can try to interest my son in becoming friendly with you? Why not mention that you would like a day at the races? He used to love going to the races, Ascot perhaps, you could have a lovely time, you know.'

Janet listened for a while then on her way to the door said, 'I will think about it, I understand what you mean.'

She managed to persuade the old lady to descend the stairs and they joined Madame who looked enquiringly at them.

'Shall we get out the cards? Surely there is some game that three can play,' said Madame.

'I would rather watch television,' said Janet and the three sat down together.

Mrs Kinder brought glasses and they passed the evening quietly after Janet had performed her usual evening journey with the car. Janet retired early, Mrs Kinder staying up as usual to help her son to bed when he came in. Janet spent some hours awake thinking over the events of the day. Obviously the two were planning to marry her off to the Captain and so obtain a housekeeper, a nurse, car driver etc. for the rest of their lives. One who could not hand in her notice to leave. What should she do? At least she had agreed on a month's trial so she had time to consider a plan of action.

She had taken the post, although all the time a thought had occurred to her that it did not seem quite an ordinary kind of job, she had never been asked for any references and there was very little actual work to do. She felt very resentful of the fact that she had scarcely a change of clothes herself and yet up in the attic there was a whole trunk full of expensive clothes which had been stored so long that they had come back into fashion again and would look really new when worn. There they were, doing nothing but just waiting to be stolen or raided by moths. Stolen! She started to think. I don't suppose they would be missed, no one ever goes up there and I don't believe that story about cold storage for the furs, they looked as if they had never been disturbed for ages. No one ever goes up there unless they are interested in becoming the wife of the Captain. The Captain! I am sure I could never marry him. He gets drunk every day, he inherits it from his mother, the liking for drink. I am sure there is no cure, just fancy, having to sleep next to that horrid drunken log every night. Fancy having to kiss that mouth, his breath must be horrible, and she got up to take a sleeping pill to obliterate the thoughts from her mind.

Next morning she was up early having breakfast with Winnie in the kitchen. Tonight, she thought, I have promised to go dancing with Jack from the garage. He seemed a nice fellow, a bit cheeky perhaps, but nice looking and tall, and about the right age, she thought. I am sick of old men, she told herself.

I wish I had a nice dress to wear, oh well, a clean blouse and skirt will have to do. 'I shall be out this evening,' she told Mrs Kinder at lunch time.

'Oh, I didn't know you knew anyone around here.'

'I am going to a dance, you don't mind if I have an evening off do you?'

'Of course not, dear,' replied Mrs Kinder, intercepting a warning glance from Madame. 'You go where you like dear, but be careful coming home by yourself at night. I wouldn't like anything to happen to you.'

Janet was walking to the garage in good time and found Jack waiting for her. He looked very smart and seemed delighted to see her. 'I'm so glad you can come,' he said and they walked to the hall together. It was a long time since Janet had been to a dance and she began to think of the days when she and Sam had first met. They had walked two miles to attend a dance in a quiet old-fashioned village and had a jolly and enjoyable time, and then had happily walked the two miles home together, enjoying every moment of the time. She felt sad and nostalgic for the first time since the terrible day that seemed almost like a bad dream now when she looked down on Sam, the Sam she had once loved, lying lifeless and bleeding on the ground. If only she could turn back the clock and start again. She had loved him, why had she left him? She must have been insane. Oh for that quiet life in that isolated cottage with no one to worry her or to want to change her life. Why did I turn against Sam? Why did I think there must be some handsome prince out there in the wide world just waiting to fall in love with me? I must try and think sanely. One had to earn the good times in life. One can't force anyone to fall in love. I may still have to accept second best or for ever remain unattached.

I must put all those thoughts behind me and try to enjoy this evening.

She found that she enjoyed both the dancing and the company. Jack was popular, everyone seemed to know him and wished her a good evening too. She was sorry when the evening was over and they started the walk home. 'Well, how did you like it?' asked Jack.

'I really did enjoy myself,' Janet replied.

'I thought you looked rather sad at times.'

'It was kind of you to take me.'

'It was a pleasure and I enjoyed myself immensely, you are a good partner, we seem to fit quite well, you are rather tall, I can't manage to dance well with a little girl. There's something I would like to ask you but I suppose I have got a bit of a cheek, after all I scarcely know you, we only met a couple of weeks ago.'

'Go on, don't make a mystery of it,' said Janet, wondering what could be coming.

'There's a dance at a small village. It's about three or four miles away but it's a grand place. They really make you welcome and we could be sure of a really good time. They had a good band, not canned music, and there will be a lot of competitions. A spot dance and quite a few really good prizes. I think you would enjoy it but there is one drawback. My car is in dock and will be for at least another fortnight. I wonder if you could borrow that car you drive for the Captain one evening? There, it's out now, I thought about it the other day and hoped to summon up the courage to ask you. Perhaps they wouldn't know if you borrowed the car?'

'Oh, I wouldn't like to do that but I don't think they would let me use if it I asked. It's not like daytime is it, and I haven't told Mrs Kinder that I know you, although she knew I was coming to the dance tonight.' Janet felt a wild desire to confide in Jack, it would be nice to tell someone of her fears and try to get someone else's opinion about the quandary she was in. She was still thinking when they arrived at her door and Janet thanked Jack and said 'Good night. I will let you know about it next week,' she said.

'I do hope we can meet again, anyway,' said Jack. 'They have dances in the hall every week.' Then he stood looking at Janet, waiting, and she began to feel that he had something to say. Then, 'May I kiss you good night?' Janet lifted her face and put her arms around his neck, she had felt so lonely and miserable at the thought of going into a friendless house and a lonely bedroom. Now, a lingering kiss seemed to give her new strength and new hope for the future.

She unlocked the door and stole quietly up to her bedroom. At least she had one good and loyal friend, she thought. She lay awake a long time wondering again, what should she do? Where could she go? There was no other home that would welcome her, she thought of her father, then of his words. She was not lying on the bed she had made for herself as he had suggested, in fact soon she would again have no bed at all.

I wonder if Jack really does care for me? I have this warm, comforting feeling when I am near him. I have never felt this before. Her thoughts rambled on. Her first sweetheart had been Sam, she had scarcely spoken to a boy before except her own brothers who had always been indifferent to her and sometimes almost cruel. She preferred to call it thoughtless. They had partly cause the rift between her father and herself, or had widened what was already there. She had loved her father, always thinking that she was his favourite child. When her own mother was ill Janet had done all she could to help him and to help her mother. One occasion stood out in her mind. She had been quite young when her mother had been taken away to hospital. 'Never mind Father,' she had said, 'I will take care of you,' and this she had every intention of doing. She knew that mother sometimes made a rice pudding and that father always seemed to enjoy it. One day she noticed that the daily delivery of milk was mounting up, she determined to make Father a rice pudding. It was made and put into the oven, according to what she remembered about the milk, sugar and rice, and getting out the dish she spooned in the rice, added the sugar and filled up the dish with milk, carefully carrying it to the oven. Time passed and, looking from time to time at the clock she decided that it would be terrible if it was not cooked. Several times she got out a tablespoon and a cup to ladle out some of the mixture to taste, to see if it was cooked. Each time it seemed to taste just the same. She suddenly noticed that the fire in the cooking range was quite low so she piled on more coal as usual then placed the dish back on the shelf.

When finally the clock indicated that it was time to prepare the table for the meal she took a final look at the pudding. The fire was by now very bright and the oven very hot. To her horror the pudding seemed to have shrunk almost all away. There were just brown, dry little seeds of rice sticking to the sides of the dish. Hastily she had removed it and put it out of sight. She had thought to be so proud of her handiwork that father would see what a good little cook she was and would let her take care of him whilst mother was away, instead of getting a woman from the village to do the housework. I love him, she had sobbed to herself, and I will show him that I can take care of him. I can make the beds and sew up a hole in his sock.

Alas, father pretended to enjoy the spoonful of dried skin and hard rice in the dish which he had insisted on seeing, and the pork pie, made by the local pork butcher which was sure to be all right anyway. He consoled his daughter saying that he did not care much for puddings anyway and that she had done her best. This was hard enough to bear but there was worse to follow. During the evening father sat down to write a letter to his wife. I will send her your love, he said to little Janet, and you can put crosses for kisses at the end. Janet thought no more about the pudding and went to bed feeling happy. Children soon forget trouble, fortunately, but next morning when father had gone to work she noticed the letter propped up on the mantelpiece. Father had left it unsealed in case he thought of anything to add before he posted it. Janet could not resist taking down the letter to look inside. There was a long account of things that had happened which meant nothing to the child until she came across her own name. Struggling to decipher the writing she made out, 'I shall be so glad when you come home dear, Janet does her best but I am sick of cold food and burnt pudding and dust everywhere, I do miss you so.' Janet had rushed upstairs and buried her burning face in father's cool pillow. 'I have let father down, he does not love me any more, what shall I do? I shall run away.' At length she had got up, even childish tears do not last long, had dried her eyes and soon forgot about it.

Well, thought Janet, all those days have gone long ago. Father does not want me any more, he has got a new wife and Sam, poor Sam is dead. Perhaps I shall be able to make a real friend of Jack, he seems a very nice fellow. Lovely thick fair hair and so tall, he is lovely to dance with. I would love to go to the dance next week. She finally fell asleep feeling more hopeful that there was indeed something left in life to live for.

Next morning Janet rose early and went down to the kitchen. Winnie was busy getting the Captain's breakfast ready. 'He has asked for an omelette today for a change,' she said. 'I am getting his tray ready.' Then as an afterthought, 'Would you like to take it up to him?'

Janet was taken aback at this suggestion then thought to herself, I suppose it would help if I tried to be nice to him, after all I do want to borrow the car if I can. 'All right,' she said and started up the stairs with the tray. She knocked on the bedroom door and entered in answer to the 'Come in' she heard. 'I have brought your breakfast today,' she said to the bloated looking figure sitting up in the bed.

'Why? Is Winnie ill?'

'No, but as usual she is very busy and I thought it would help her,' Janet replied. 'How are you today?'

'How do I know?' was the growled reply. 'Ask me again later, I don't suppose you really want to know anyway, nobody cares how I am.'

'Oh yes they do. Your mother cares very much and I am sure Winnie does, look at the care she has taken with your breakfast tray and your mother would be very happy if you stayed at home sometimes for your lunch.'

'Oh no! I see she has roped you in to try to keep me away from the club, has she?'

'No, she has not,' replied Janet. 'I care and would like to help you if you would let me.'

'All right, that will do, you can go now,' he replied rather rudely.

Janet had her breakfast and went to clean the car windows and get it ready. He is a bad tempered, surly fellow, she thought, but if I want to stay here I must try to keep on good terms with him, at least to make sure that his mother thinks he likes me.

The old village dance was only a few days away and Janet called at the garage after taking the Captain to his club to try to see Jack. He seemed to be investigating something under the bonnet of a car but looked pleased to see her. Wiping his hands he came forward and asked if she had fixed up to borrow the car for the dance.

'No, I haven't asked yet,' replied Janet, 'but I feel sure that it will be all right.' She looked at the smiling face of the mechanic and thought how nice it would be to see him coming home to greet her at the end of the day. They could have a little cottage in a country village with a petrol filling station at its side and a small repair shop. How happy she could be with someone like him. She could keep hens in a field at the rear and could hatch chickens. Perhaps there will be a stream and they could have ducks.

Janet suddenly realized where she was and that Jack was standing looking at her and that she was daydreaming. 'I will ask her today, you have not told me where you live, perhaps I could call round and tell you what she says.'

Jack replied rather cautiously, 'You can usually find me here.'

Janet took this for a rebuff and got into the car at once and drove away.

After lunch Mrs Kinder and Madame were talking about going for a drive and Janet thought at least this is an innovation. Mrs Kinder had always disappeared after lunch and seldom reappeared until the next meal was due. 'Would you like me to drive you out when I have brought the Captain homed this afternoon?' asked Janet.

'That would be lovely,' Madame at once replied and Mrs Kinder agreed. 'We can be ready by three o'clock,' she said.

When Janet came back downstairs from helping the Captain up to his room for his afternoon sleep the two ladies were waiting for her. All through the afternoon the two ladies sat in the back of the car talking and Janet could not think why they wanted to ride in the car at all, they could just as easily have carried on that conversation at home and more comfortably, Janet thought. She spent most of the time trying to sum up enough courage to ask if she could borrow the car on Friday evening but when the car finally drew up in front of the house she had not said anything about it. She made up her mind to ask the Captain tonight, he was usually in a good mood after his afternoon rest. After tea she started to think about a dress for the dance. How she wished that she could borrow one of the models she had seen in the trunk in the attic. Surely Jack would fall in love with her if he saw her looking really glamorous. 'Why not?' she asked herself. Surely if she was careful and put it back again intact there would be no reason for anyone to know that it had been out of the trunk. I will go up there tomorrow afternoon when the house is quiet and get one out. There was a lovely midnight blue long dress trimmed with sequins there, I do hope it will fit me, she said to herself.

When the time came to take the Captain to his club Janet helped him carefully into the car and asked if he was comfortable. During the short journey she talked about the afternoon drive and he said, 'You like driving don't you? And you drive very well I must say.'

Janet felt very pleased to find the Captain in a good mood and replied, 'Yes, I wish I had a car of my own again.'

'I am sure you could use this one any time you wanted it, in moderation of course,' he replied.

Janet could scarcely hide her excitement. 'Do you really mean that? As a matter of fact I would like to borrow it on Friday evening, I have been invited out.'

'I was not aware that you had any friends in the district, I didn't mean a long journey, you know.'

'Oh no,' replied Janet hastily, 'it is only to a village near here to see someone.'

'Very well then, but perhaps it would be better if you said nothing to Mother about it.'

Janet did not very much like the turn the conversation had taken, but she had permission to use the car. She could scarcely wait to tell Jack but knew that the garage would be closed.

During the night her thoughts turned again to her loneliness and longing for love. I believe Jack is rather interested in me, she thought. I feel that I could really love him if given the chance, and fell asleep to dream of him.

Next day she took the Captain to his club as usual and called at the garage on her way back. 'Jack, I have got permission to use the car tomorrow night.'

'Good,' said Jack, 'I tell you what, we could take a pal of mine and his girlfriend with us if you like. I usually pick them up when I take my car, you wouldn't mind would you?'

Janet's face fell, she felt as if a shower of cold water had fallen over her excited face. 'Of course not,' she found herself replying, although that was far from how she felt. The evening would be spoilt if she had to share the company of the handsome Jack with others. She felt disconsolate and disappointed. She had built up such a picture of happiness throughout the evening with Jack for company all the time. Now I must make the best of it, she realized. The thought occurred to her that she could say that the car was not available after all, but why punish herself? She had looked forward so much to Jack's company and had to admit to herself that it was this rather than the dance that had sounded so attractive.

The house was very quiet as Janet stole quietly up the attic stairs. Opening the huge trunk she took out the first garment. It was a red velvet evening jacket. Looking further she found a midnight blue voile evening dress, trimmed with tiny silver beads. The sleeves were full and shaped like wings, the full skirt hung gracefully over the satin lining. This is my colour, she delightedly told herself, I must have this. The velvet jacket was a temptation but thinking of Jack and the likelihood that his friends might be more soberly dressed she settled for the dress and left the jacket in the trunk. What a pity there are no shoes, she thought, but I must be satisfied with this lovely dress. I suppose I shall have to let Jack drive the car. Then she listened carefully and made sure there was no one about, then went quietly down the attic stairs and into her own room. Hanging up the dress in the back of the wardrobe she spent the rest of the evening in delightful anticipation. 'I shall have to come back to change after taking the Captain to his club, and I hope that no one will be around, it is usually quiet in the evening.

* * *

Everything went as planned the next evening and she called at the garage by arrangement to collect Jack then on to the home of his friend. A tall young man stepped into the car and pointed out another house in the vicinity, in the doorway stood a girl. She was short and rather plump and very poorly dressed. For the first time Janet had misgivings about her dress. It now seemed rather elaborate for a country village dance. It was too late to do anything about that now and the car sped on in Jack's capable hands.

The hall was sparkling with light and the sound of music floated out on the night air to set the toes tingling. They parked the car and hurried into the hall.

Emerging from the cloakroom Janet had mixed feelings. She was proud of her lovely dress but all eyes seemed to her to be focused in her direction. She could not stem the feeling of exultation as Jack led her gracefully on to the floor to the music of a graceful old-fashioned waltz. It was a spot dance and somehow Janet knew that they were going to be lucky, they were. Sure enough Janet's shoe covered the pre-arranged spot and amidst much clapping the two received their prizes. Jack looked quite flushed and happy as they continued the dance. It seemed to be a lovely evening and, tired as she was, Janet wished that it could go on for ever. Eventually the last dance was announced and there was a rush to get coats. Jack brought the car round to the door and the two girls, who had scarcely had a chance to speak to each other all night, were soon in the car and on the way home. Jack suggested that his friends could be taken home first and then he could take Janet home, leave the car there and walk home.

'Where do you live?' asked Janet. She had thought for a start that he was the owner of the garage business and had been surprised when another man had appeared who was more probably the owner. 'You would not be very interested in my home,' he said. 'It's only a cottage. I live with my mother.'

'You are wrong there, I would love to meet your mother and I love pretty cottages,' replied Janet.

'It is not a pretty cottage with roses round the door, we are not idle rich you know, we can't choose where to live, we have to make the best of whatever we can get.'

Janet had been hoping all through the evening that Jack would make some effort to get more closely acquainted with her, he had seemed so anxious to be friendly, or perhaps rather more than friendly, ever since she had first made his acquaintance at the garage. She had made an effort to fix up transport for this evening and perhaps she had let her own thoughts and wishes lead her into thinking that Jack was interested in her. Outside the garage at the house they sat in the car, Janet hoping that Jack would make some kind of suggestion about another meeting or at least kiss her good night, but he seemed anxious to get away.

Jack left the car with mixed feelings, he had been completely surprised when Janet walked out of the cloakroom sparkling with what looked to him like diamonds, rubies and emeralds. Even if not real, he thought, they must have cost a small fortune. A beautiful dress, looking like a dream, or like some fashionable film actress. Janet must either be very rich or a very skilful liar, or both he thought. He had not really noticed her everyday appearance. To him her clothes had looked the same as those worn by any other local girl. He remembered how she had been worried at the village dance in case her clothes were not good enough, she had in fact looked a little shabby he had thought, to his inexperienced eyes. Then to suddenly appear dressed like a film star, also with a string of pearls, a bracelet and what looked like a gold wrist watch, the latter he felt sure he had never seen before. She had most surely been, to use his own expression, leading him on. He told himself that he would be a fool to suppose that he could keep up with a girlfriend as rich as she must be. The mere thought of taking her home and introducing her to his mother made him tremble with horror. He decided that it was best to discourage any further friendliness. He was disappointed and sorry. He had thought that a really lovely girl had come into his life. She had laughed and joked with him and seemed to seek his company, even to enjoy it. He said 'Good night' although it was nearly morning and walked thoughtfully home.

10

Janet could not understand why Jack had changed so suddenly last night. She had been so eager to please him and had ventured to think that at last she had met a true friend who was really interested in her and might grow to love her.

Jack had been rather shy as a boy. He had no sisters and looked upon girls as an unknown quantity. He had grown into a very presentable young man and his position at the garage had brought him into contact with many women of all ages and circumstances. He had been patronized, flattered and treated very rudely in turn. On reflection he thought that the most insulting behaviour had been handed out to him by a titled lady who called sometimes for petrol, oil or tyre inflation. She would sit in the car looking at him with a glance enough to wither, he thought, whilst he attended to her car, then she would throw a coin out of the car window and watch him pick it up. He had only stooped to do this once, that time he had been so surprised that it had been automatic. After that time he had just left the coin in the mud and had walked away. All this went through his mind as he walked home and he grew more and more angry at each step. To think that she had the cheek to let me pay for her evening out and to make such a fuss about thanking me. She could have paid for the lot of us and never would have missed the money.

Whilst this was going through Jack's mind as he walked a greater turmoil was working in Janet's head. What have I done? I went to a great deal of trouble to borrow a car, and even a risk to borrow a dress so that I would not let Jack down in front of his friends and all the evening he has treated me as if I would break or collapse, how different the evening has been to the friendly 'hop' in the village hall last week. We were happy together then, he seemed so nice, what have I done? I wonder if I have got bad breath? Why am I fated to choose the wrong one every time? What is love anyway? I thought I loved Sam for a while until I found that living with him was impossible. He was almost like an animal at times. When he ate, food slopped out of his mouth and fell on his clothes. He never wanted to have a bath. I can never forget the first few weeks of my married life with him. To see great crusts of bread and cheese in his open mouth. To hear the awful sounds he made as he drank, to see him spit into the fire, Janet shuddered at the recollections.

He could not help his upbringing and was kind in his own way. I recall the first time he came in from a cold walk around the sheep with a tiny bunch of violets in his cold hand. I think that horrible sheep insect was the final straw, I shudder now when I think of it burrowing into my clothes. He loved me though, and I hurt him terribly. How I wish I could undo what I did to him. Father knew that my life would be very different if I married Sam and I defied him. I wonder if ever I shall see father again and if his new wife is making him happy. Then I had to go and fall in love with Will, I really did think he loved me. He was prepared to give up his wife and start a new home with me. We had lovely times in bed. I was sure he loved me at the time. How could anyone do all of those things if they were not in love? Surely that was all a part of being in love. Perhaps he really is a nice man and found that his wife was so miserable without him that he had no right to be happy with me. It must be myself that is wrong and unlucky.

Then Arthur, why did I feel so sick when he came into my bedroom and tried to kiss me in bed? Perhaps it is the fate of women to either live a solitary life or to become the servant or plaything of any man who happens to think that he would like to live with her. I must have it all wrong. What is love? Is it a fleeting thing, I wonder? It cannot always be like this, what about the golden weddings one reads about in newspapers? Two people must at least have found some kind of happiness to have lived together all those years and still be happy together. Try as she might to sleep, Janet could not and when morning dawned she was hollowed-eyed and had a terrible headache. She found it difficult to face Winnie in the kitchen and could not take more than a cup of tea at breakfast time. Winnie was waiting to hear all about the dance but Janet would say nothing except, 'It was all right but now I have got a terrible headache.'

'Too much to drink I expect,' stated Winnie wisely and went to get a headache pill. 'Here, take this, you can tell me all about it later, do you know I was quite jealous of you when I saw you go off from my window. I was not spying on you but I did hope that you would have come into my room to show me your dress before you went, what colour is it?'

Janet didn't know what to say, Winnie had been a good friend and was always kind, but she hesitated to take her into her confidence about the evening dress. Winnie was intensely loyal to her mistress and Janet admired her for it.

It was almost time to take the Captain to his club and Janet went into the garage to make sure that the car was clean and tidy. She had once heard a story about a woman who had found a bra on the back seat of her husband's car one morning and in that story the husband had difficulty in persuading her that it was a cleaning cloth he had picked up somewhere. There was nothing in the car and it looked remarkably clean as she opened the door for the Captain.

'How did you enjoy yourself last night?' he asked. 'I wish I was a bit more spry on my feet, I would have taken you to one of our Company dinners. Would you have come with me?'

'I enjoyed myself very much thank you,' said Janet. 'As for the dinner you spoke of, I expect I would have enjoyed being a guest.'

The Captain leaned towards Janet as she got into the driver's seat. 'It's not too late you know,' he said, leaning towards her and smiling into her face.

She was rather surprised to find that he suddenly looked entirely different. The pale, pasty face with the nautical beard suddenly lit up. The mouth lost its sarcastic twist and a warm smile spread across his face. His eyes twinkled and Janet felt a warm glow stealing over her whole body. She started the engine and tried to concentrate on driving and on the car.

'You see I did not harm the car after all,' she said.

'Of course you didn't and you can borrow it any time. You had better ask me first though, as Mother might object. I might even come with you,' he finished, and Janet suspected that he was indulging in a joke at her expense.

'I hardly think that visiting in a village would be your idea of an evening out,' said Janet. Just in time she reminded herself that he had agreed for her to use the car to visit friends. He might have felt differently if he had known that she was taking people to a dance in it.

'What do you think I would call an enjoyable evening out then?' The Captain leaned closer and smiled into her face. Janet tried to think of a non-committal answer. 'You could take me out one afternoon or I could book seats for a show. God damn it, though, I expect my mother would want to come too, not to speak of that propped up travesty of a dancing doll she has roped in to stay with her.'

Janet could not help a chuckle, the remarks were made in such a spontaneous way. She was very surprised to find what a different man the Captain was now that he seemed to have discarded his hard, bad-mannered shell. Janet wondered which was the real man, was it the drink that made him sour and so bad tempered, or was he in pain, and did he take the drink to try to ease the pain? Or the third alternative, was he naturally a bad-tempered man who could turn on the charm when he liked? The latter would be the most dangerous, she thought. She decided to see if Winnie knew anything about the Captain's past when she had an opportunity. When they arrived at the club, instead of going in to fetch someone out to help the Captain to mount the steps he said, 'Stay a minute, I think I could manage with your help to get up the steps, I am much better today,' and he took hold of Janet's arm and leaned on her rather heavily, apologizing profusely. The went into the club and one or two faces were turned, looking surprised. 'Hello Major,' the Captain said to a gentleman with rather a red face sitting facing the entrance. 'Come and meet my friend Miss Smith, she is staying with my mother and is good enough to drive me to the club sometimes.'

'Hullo, I am pleased to see that Percy has got a lady friend at last,' said the Major, taking Janet's hand and gripping it hard. Janet felt the hot colour slowly creeping over her face and neck. Really, this was too bad, a lady friend indeed! She turned and left the club rather abruptly and could not resist driving by the garage, she decided that the tank would take a couple of gallons of petrol and she drove the car by the pump and stopped. Usually Jack would spot her and would be ready with a smile but today the young boy who had recently started there came forward.

'Is Mr Willard not at work today?'

'Yes Miss, he is busy under a car, I can serve you. Do you want him?'

'No, it's all right, carry on.'

Janet felt angry at this pointed snub.

'What have I done?' she again asked herself. There's only one way to find out, ask him. But somehow she found it difficult to put into words what she wanted to ask. She took the car home and the thought came into her head that perhaps the Captain would not make too bad a husband after all, perhaps she would not have to sleep with him, at least she would have a nice home, a car, and someone to wait on her, and oh yes, a mother-in-law. She shuddered again at the thought of being trapped in this dull suburban house with a drunken husband and a mother-in-law for the rest of her life. She began to wonder if her natural dislike of the smell of alcohol was caused by her own abstinence. She had been brought up in a family that, although they were not quite teetotal, drank white wine only at Christmas or to celebrate some special occasion. She had never taken anything intoxicating in her life but began to wonder if it was very silly to avoid all except the small glass of weak sherry that Mrs Kinder poured out for her. So many people seemed to gain so much pleasure from it. She decided that when Mrs Kinder asked her to have a second glass she would take it in future.

Lunchtime soon came round and she was surprised to hear the telephone ring. This seldom happened at any time and never before lunch. She picked up the receiver and was surprised to hear the Captain's voice. 'Hallo my dear, will you tell Winnie to set another place at table and bring the car for me, I have decided to come home for lunch.'

'All right, I'll come for you right away.' Janet went to tell Winnie and called to Mrs Kinder who was talking in her guest's bedroom.

'He's coming home to lunch? I don't believe it, tell Winnie to lay another place and to open some tinned fruit. That pie won't be nearly enough for a sweet.'

'Don't worry,' said Janet. 'There will be plenty, there is always something left over anyway,' and she hurried off to get the car out calling to Winnie on the way.

I wonder if his new attitude to me is anything to do with this decision, she thought, she was not long in finding out. She drew the car up outside the club as usual and expected the doors to open and for the Captain, helped along by a waiter, to appear. Instead the doors remained closed and she sat for a few minutes waiting. When nothing seemed to happen she thought that after all it was not the usual time and so I suppose they are waiting for me to announce that the car is here. Accordingly she entered the club. There sat the Captain at a small table, a drink at his elbow and face to face with the Major. He waved and pointed to a third chair at the table and waited for her to come and sit there. 'What will you have to drink?' he asked, and Janet opened her mouth to say as usual 'I don't drink thank you', but a sudden recollection of her earlier thinking flashed into her mind.

'I will have whatever you are having,' she said, not knowing what else to say.

'I don't think somehow that you would like whiskey,' the Captain said, 'Why not a sweet sherry?' and Janet said 'Thank you' and went to sit in the chair.

'Sweet to the sweet,' said the Major.

'Don't take any notice of him,' said the Captain, 'he has been knocking it back all morning.'

Both the men laughed and as the steward went to get the drink Janet laughed too. 'Why not?' she asked herself. She was agreeably surprised to find that she enjoyed the drink and began to regret that she had always obstinately refused to accept the offer of anything like that in the past. 'I suppose I shall be lighting up a cigarette next,' she remarked jocularly.

'I can't help you there,' said the Captain, 'I don't smoke and neither does Ronnie.'

Janet was surprised to find that the Captain seemed much more steady than usual on his feet and almost managed to walk to the car alone. They arrived home in good time for lunch and Mrs Kinder came to the door beaming with pleasure. 'How nice to see you dear, I am so glad you could get home for lunch, I am afraid we have nothing very exciting, you should have given me more notice, Winnie would gladly have prepared something more exciting for you.'

'Don't worry,' replied the Captain gallantly, 'I shall enjoy the company of you three ladies more than the food.'

The four seated themselves and Winnie appeared looking happy and excited with the soup. She also looked as if she was pleased to have the pleasure of cooking for four for a change.

When the coffee stage was reached the Captain surprised everyone by saying 'What about a drive this afternoon? It's a nice day and we have a first-class driver in our company, that is if she does not mind,' he added hastily.

'Oh no, I would love to drive you all out but I don't know this part of the country very well.'

'What about going to Chatsworth?' asked Madame Susette.

'I think there would be too much walking there,' put in Mrs Kinder. 'My son is after all not quite his old self yet.'

'Have you been to Chatsworth?' she asked Janet.

'Oh yes, I was absolutely fascinated with the painting of that violin which seems so real that one could actually feel sure that it was a real instrument hanging on the door, with the bow across it.'

'I don't remember that,' said Mrs Kinder, 'but I am sure we would all enjoy looking at it and if Percy finds walking too difficult he could sit in the car, it is a lovely day and it would be nice to enjoy fresh air for a change.'

'All right,' said Janet, 'I will go and get ready and see if the car is all right for a journey.'

'It's rather a long way for her to drive, don't you think?' volunteered the Captain.

'Oh no,' put in Janet, 'I love driving and it is such an easy car to drive. We will have to fill the tank before we start and have the car checked round.'

'Of course,' said Mrs Kinder, 'we can do that on the way.'

They all dispersed and left Winnie to clear the table and to attend to her usual work.

It was a nice day and Jack came out looking rather surprised when they reached the garage. He had never seen four occupants in the car before except when he happened to be the driver a few days ago. Janet got out of the car and went to watch as he fed the petrol into the tank. 'Are you going to the usual dance on Friday?' she asked quickly.

Jack looked the other way and seemed reluctant to meet her glance. 'I am surprised that a lady like you wants to dance with the likes of me actually,' he muttered between his teeth.

'I don't know what has got into you,' said Janet. 'You were anxious enough for me to come last time.'

By this time the tank was full and there was no excuse to linger any longer. Janet got back into the driver's seat and started the car. Oh well, she thought, he had either got someone else or I have offended him in some way.

It was a very enjoyable afternoon for all four and the Captain seemed to have a new lease of life, he managed to walk around the house and to stand with the three ladies to marvel at the painting of the violin which appeared to be hanging, together with its bow, on a hook on a door. Unfortunately the door was at the back of the room and somewhat in shadow. A thick cord was stretched across the room to keep visitors from getting close to the door to examine the painting. It was very difficult to believe that it was not a real violin and bow hanging there. The two ladies went afterwards to look around the garden and the Captain said that he would sit in the car.

'What about you?' he asked Janet.

'I will sit with you if you like, I have already seen the grounds although it is some time ago, I shall be pleased to sit and rest for a while. I was out rather late recently and have not quite recovered.'

Mrs Kinder looked rather searchingly at her but made no remark and Janet wished that she had kept quiet about her use of the car. She left the rear seat to the Captain who had brought along the *Daily Telegraph* which he proceeded to lose himself in. Before very long Janet could hear faint snores coming from behind the paper and had no compunction in discarding the *A.A.* magazine that she had been idly glancing through and sitting back with eyes closed herself. This is a very pleasant way to spend an afternoon, she mused, although not very exciting. She had been awake so long during the night that she had difficulty in keeping awake. What should I do? she asked herself again, none of the people that she had met recently were aware that she had been married. She was still not twenty years of age but felt much older. Not old enough however, she told herself, to spend the rest of her life looking after tired old people. I want some excitement and pleasure out of life. Surely I have not got to pay all the rest of my life for the wicked and foolish things I have done in the past. I must not blame Father, he had every right to be ashamed of me but if he had been a little more tolerant I think I would have made more of an effort to make my marriage work, but all that is in the past now. Oh, if only I could meet someone that I could love and who would love me. I need some love, love and affection. How can I go on living in such a cold and non-caring atmosphere? I wouldn't mind being poor, or even living in an isolated place or even being lonely sometimes if only I had someone to love. If my baby had lived I would have had something to do and someone to love, someone that returned my love and care. She drew a mutual picture of herself wheeling her little son out for a walk.

Then she stopped herself dreaming with the thought, we couldn't have afforded a decent pram anyway, it would have been someone else's old one I suppose. Oh, what's the use of dreaming? Suddenly she was aware of voices. It was Mrs Kinder and her friend returning. She began to cough loudly hoping that the Captain would wake up. He was soundly asleep however and his mother said, 'What a shame, poor dear. He has tired himself out with all that walking. He is still not very strong you know,' and to Janet, 'Why don't you come for a little walk with us? We may be able to get some ices or a cup of tea.'

Janet agreed and the three strolled around, Janet thinking she could not stand a life as deadly boring as this for always. This should help me to make up my mind, but I must try and see Jack and have a talk with him, I can't understand why he has changed so suddenly unless he has found another girl. I wish I knew where he lives, he seemed to be ashamed to tell me.

During the drive home Janet made up her mind to see Jack at all costs even if she asked someone where he lived.

The three arrived home tired but happy. Janet put the car away having been told that the Captain would not be going to the club tonight. They would like to play bridge at home but unfortunately Janet could not play, she said that she had heard of it but had no idea how to play. 'You must learn,' said Madame, 'all good people play bridge these days, besides it would keep the Captain at home in the evening if he could have some bridge practice here.'

She prevailed upon Janet to sit with the three and to try to learn something of the game. They would tell her what to do. Janet had no wish to learn but could not avoid trying to and the rest of the evening soon passed.

After more thought Janet decided that she really must see Jack and she wrote a note and stole quietly out of the house when all had retired and walked along the deserted street to the garage. She had stated that she really must see Jack, she had something very important to say to him. She would be passing the garage next evening and named a time. She knew that the garage would be closed now and that it would be quite convenient to call there tomorrow on her return journey from the Captain's club. She anticipated that he would want to take her as usual the next day. She dropped the note through the letter box and hoped that it would have the desired effect. After all Jack owed it to her to explain why he had suddenly decided to end their friendship.

That night Janet slept soundly, she felt quite worn out mentally and physically. It seemed to be morning all too soon and Winnie arrived with a cup of tea saying, 'It is eight o'clock, I could see that you were overtired last night and thought you might oversleep so I brought you a cup of tea.'

'How kind you are Winnie,' Janet said.

'Well, you might be my mistress one day I suppose, the Captain seems to be getting quite fond of you, I don't ever remember him staying away from the club all evening or even coming home to lunch.' The girl looked very happy to say this.

'Oh I don't know about that,' said Janet, 'I would have to love someone before I could consent to marry them.'

'Yes, of course,' said Winnie and hurriedly retired from the bedroom.

The Captain made his usual visit to the club before lunch and returned to rest for the afternoon. He re-established his evening visit also for which Janet was pleased. After leaving him at his club at seven pm she drove the car by the garage and Jack was waiting there. He climbed into the front seat next to her and started, 'Hallo Janet, what was it you wanted to see me about?'

'I would have thought you might know, why have you been avoiding me? We were good friends until we all went to that dance. If it is because I didn't say much to your friends it was not my fault. They both seemed to avoid me all through the evening. You suddenly seemed to turn against me when I asked you where you lived. I am not a suspicious person but it seems strange to me that you want to keep your home a secret from me, what is the mystery? Is there someone there you don't want me to meet?'

Jack sat quietly looking ahead for a few moments then said 'If you must know I think you are above me in station. It's not that I am ashamed of my home or of my mother, I really thought that you were just the girl I had been waiting for, then you turned up at that dance wearing a dress fit to kill. It must have cost a small fortune. All those diamonds or whatever they were, then the jewellery. There isn't a bat's chance in hell that I would ever afford to keep a wife that was used to that kind of life. You have never spoken about your parents, they must be titled people at least. There were pearls and rings, they were obviously gold, then a bracelet, and a watch. Then you asked where I lived. Then I said in a small cottage and you said you loved little cottages. Love little cottages my foot! Love big mansions you mean.'

Here Jack paused for breath and Janet said, 'Have you finished?'

'Isn't that enough?'

'Yes, quite enough, and I think you are priceless. The dress was borrowed, the jewellery also, most of it, the pearls were my mother's, she has been dead a long time. The watch was a present from my father for passing an exam in music and for trying to look after him when my mother died.'

Janet suddenly stopped talking. Jack had taken her into his arms as well as he could in the cramped front seat of the car with the gear lever in the way.

'Now let me tell you about my mother and our cottage, she is very particular you see, I am all she has got left, she would like to meet you really, I started to tell her about you, then when I thought you were above me in station I told her that you had gone away. I would not like her to get hurt, I am terribly sorry if I have hurt you. When I first saw you I think I fell in love, you seemed to be just the right girl for me, so clean and young and innocent. I was longing to kiss you after that first dance you came to in the hall but I could scarcely believe my luck and I was afraid of offending you.'

The two sat talking for so long that they lost all sense of time, suddenly Janet said, 'I must take the car back, they will wonder where I have got to.'

'Will you be able to come to the dance on Friday evening at the hall then, my own darling?' asked Jack.

Scarcely able to contain her joy and relief Janet agreed and they parted reluctantly.

Janet put the car away and went straight to her bedroom her eyes like stars. At last she had met the right one, the only one.

Tall, handsome, kind, and what was more, he loved her. She was in heaven, she longed for the next day to dawn and to pass. It was Friday and she could not wait for the evening. She was walking on air and would dance the evening away in her old blouse and skirt. At least it was clean, and no jewellery, just her watch, he understood about the watch.

11

'I want to talk to you,' said Mrs Kinder on Friday morning. 'I never seem to be able to find you these days, come and sit down here in my room.'

Janet felt a kind of premonition. Had Mrs Kinder discovered that she had borrowed the dress?

'I am sorry, I seem to have been rather busy and actually I have had an awfully bad headache these last two days. I think it must have been the sun on the day we went to Chatsworth.'

'I am sorry to hear that, why didn't you say? I could have found something for you, my dear. I want to talk to you about my son. He has really taken to you and I am so pleased. He seems a new man. It has given him new hope meeting you. Madame says you two are made for each other and that she saw it coming as soon as she put the idea into your head. You have been very clever my dear, most young ladies would have thrown themselves at his head. That would have been disastrous, he would have retired even further into his shell.'

Into his club you mean, Janet could not help thinking. She had been trying vainly to get a word in during this conversation. The right words just would not come. What shall I do? she thought, almost in a panic. At length Mrs Kinder paused to draw breath.

Janet said, 'Will you excuse me, I feel quite faint, I have had this headache for several days and I would like to lie down quietly for an hour or so.'

'All right dear, I quite understand, you have a rest then I want to talk to you about money. The ridiculous arrangement we made about salary is silly now. You must have all you want to spend on clothes etc. Don't be offended dear, but I have noticed you have let your things get quite shabby haven't you?

We must come to some arrangement about that. I can take you shopping. Oh! All right dear, sorry, I don't want to worry you if you are poorly. Would you like to see the doctor if I send for him?'

'Oh no Mrs Kinder, please, please let me have a rest my head is throbbing.'

'All right dear I understand. I will leave you to have a lie down.'

Thank heaven for that, thought Janet. I don't know what I am going to do. I shall have to confide in Jack and see what he has got to say. She rested for an hour, appearing only in time to take the Captain to his club. 'We must have another afternoon out sometime,' he said. 'Not tomorrow or Sunday, places are too crowded with the rabble. We will see how it goes on Monday shall we?'

'All right,' said Janet and omitted with difficulty the word Sir. I must not offend him now, she thought, I might want the car again. When they arrived at the club the Captain opened the car door himself and got out saying, 'Would you like to come in for a drink my dear?'

Janet declined, saying that she had a bad head.

'See you later then,' he replied.

Janet drove hurriedly away. How am I going to manage to get to that dance tonight without arousing suspicion? Last time she was out for the evening Madame asked where she had been and wanted to know if Mrs Kinder was aware that she had been out late. Janet had replied that she was not aware that anyone had the right to order her comings and goings at any time. She spent the afternoon re-arranging the flowers in the house, she was not afraid of finding anyone about. Everyone always seemed to go to sleep every afternoon, emerging again in time for the next meal. Winnie sometimes had to take a cup of tea up to her mistress's bedroom and sometimes Janet joined Winnie in the kitchen for tea. Occasionally the pair had been venturesome and had made toast or Welsh rarebit and had enjoyed it together like conspirators. Janet like the little maid very much and longed to share her new happiness with her but she knew that it would be dangerous to tell the girl about Jack. She would certainly disapprove, her loyalty to her employer would come first. Although the Captain was often rude to her with hurtful remarks about the food she admired him and would cheerfully put up with rude remarks which were all forgiven and forgotten at the sight of his smile.

Janet was ready with the car at the usual time in the evening and to her relief the Captain seemed to be in a sullen mood and scarcely spoke to her. She put the car away and entered the dining room. Winnie was just putting finishing touches to the table. The ladies came down and admired the arrangement of fresh flowers, Winnie brought in the soup and the meal started in silence. As soon as the coffee appeared Janet declined her usual cup and rising to leave the table she asked to be excused, saying nothing more and making no excuse. She had already dressed in her neat blouse and skirt, she changed her shoes, put on a coat and hurriedly left the house. Jack was waiting for her outside and the two walked to the dance hall together. 'I am so pleased that we have got that horrid misunderstanding cleared up,' Janet said, 'but I am very worried about my job. Mrs Kinder seems to think that the Captain would like to marry me and she would heartily disapprove if she knew where I am and what I am doing tonight.'

'Well, we can't help that,' said Jack. 'And it's none of her business anyway, she hasn't bought you body and soul.'

'No, I know that, but I expect she would ask me to leave if she got to know that I had a boyfriend.'

'You have every right to choose what friends you like.'

'Yes, I know, but you don't understand, what she really wants in the house is a wife for her son, not a companion.'

'She jolly well won't get one then, will she? At least she won't get you, if you become anybody's wife it will be mine. By the way, I have told Mother about you and she would like to meet you. You are invited to tea on Sunday. Well, what have I said now? I thought you would be pleased.'

'Yes, of course I am pleased,' said Janet. 'I am delighted, I have looked forward very much to meeting your mother but it will cause consternation if I say where I am going.'

'Why, for goodness sake?' said Jack angrily.

'Please try to understand, I shall be out of a job if she realizes that I am not interested in her son.'

'I don't understand, I am afraid. Did she tell you that when she engaged her?'

'No, of course not, or I would not have taken the job.'

'Where did you work before and why did you leave?'

Janet told him about the farmer and his son. By now they had reached the dance hall and the conversation was forgotten in the excitement of meeting Jack's friends, both male and female. Janet had noticed before how popular Jack was. Several girls came up to him and said that they hoped that Jack would have a dance with them during the evening. Gradually a feeling grew in Janet's mind that she had never felt before. She found herself watching Jack and listening for his replies. She compared him with some of the other young men in the hall and considered that he was easily the best looking young man there. She tried to define the feeling she had when other girls addressed him, was it jealousy? Was she really falling in love for the very first time?

She had never felt possessive about Sam, she had never cared where he was or what he was doing. Then she thought of Will, what she had felt for him she had thought was love, she had enjoyed his company and shared his bed and he had aroused in her a certain enjoyment of contact with him, but she had never cared who he was with when away from her or what he was doing — only in the sense that she had disliked being left alone in a strange place where she knew no one. This feeling she was just beginning to experience seemed possessive. She hated the thought that Jack could even look at another girl. She enjoyed the dances she and Jack had together and when another young man asked her for a dance she refused, thinking that it would give some other girl the chance to dance with Jack if she left him alone for a while. She had never felt like this before and was rather apprehensive of what the effect might be if Jack recognized her possessiveness. She had astonished herself by her feelings and her reaction, when he had suddenly seemed to turn cold and uninterested in her, but she had no further cause for worry during the rest of the evening. They were familiar with all the dances, it was a new band that all agreed was much more satisfactory than canned music. The fellows in the band seemed to join in the fun and several competitions were staged. Jack and Janet won the fun prize which was for a couple with a lady wearing blue panties. Janet felt very shy when the M.C. announced the details and whispered to Jack that she could fulfil the requirements but she did not wish to be named. Jack at once shot up his hand and claimed the prize, a large ripe melon. 'This will do for Mother if you agree,' he said. 'She loves them.'

'Please don't tell her how you acquired it,' begged Janet.

The walk home in the cool night air was the last pleasure of a wonderful evening. Janet felt that at last her cup of happiness was full. They parted after a lingering goodbye kiss having agreed that Janet should go to his home to meet his mother for tea on Sunday.

Janet lay in bed thinking very different thoughts to those that kept her awake two nights ago. Then she seemed to have no one in the world to turn to for help, advice or friendship. Now she had a loving sweetheart, a prospective mother-in-law and quite a host of jolly friends. She put aside any recurring feelings of jealousy of other girls. Of course Jack was popular, she told herself, he had lived all his life in the neighbourhood. If he had wished to find a sweetheart amongst the village girls he had plenty from which to choose. He preferred her, and with that comfortable assurance she went to sleep.

Next morning she resumed her duties feeling much brighter and happier. The Captain noticed her happy smiling face and remarked that she looked good and obviously felt better. She supposed that he was not aware that she had been out the evening before and began to plan what she should say when Mrs Kinder asked where she had been and tried to resume the embarrassing conversation of the day before. She assured herself that she had a right to go where she liked but still felt very sensitive when asked.

To her relief the Captain did not ask her to join him in the club and when she got back to the house the ladies had not appeared. She went about her usual light duties trying to avoid talking to Winnie who she knew was longing to ask her how she had enjoyed her evening. Reading between the lines Janet felt sure that she knew what Winnie's next request would be, she would want to go to the local dances.

Lunch was a leisurely meal and Janet found an excuse to leave the table immediately and did not appear again after fetching the Captain from the club. Against her own inclinations she went for a long walk. She had to think, she could not make any plans for the future until she had discussed her position with Jack. It was very clear that she would not be able to keep her job with the Kinders once they discovered that she had a regular man friend. Obviously all Mrs Kinder's plans centred around finding a suitable wife for her son, ably assisted by Madame who had obviously been invited to the house with the object of helping to further the plan. Janet was relieved when Saturday was over and on Sunday morning the first time she encountered anyone was on her first trip to the club with the Captain. He seemed to have slipped back into his morose attitude and said, 'See you about two thirty.'

During lunch Mrs Kinder asked if Janet would like to go for a drive in the country. Janet had been dreading something like this and knew that it had to come. 'No,' she replied. 'I am going out.'

'Where?' asked Mrs Kinder promptly. 'I was not aware that you knew anyone locally, or have you been keeping something from me?'

Janet was at a loss for words.

'I had something I wanted to say to you and I had made plans for this afternoon. Madame and I have been thinking out an arrangement we would like to discuss with you, it concerns money and could be very much to your advantage.'

'Oh yes? You know you are quite wrong about the Captain, I am sure he has no wish to marry, he seems quite happy with his way of life and his friends at the club.'

'You know nothing about it,' snapped Mrs Kinder. 'Whether he likes it or not, he has got to put a stop to this heavy drinking and the best way is to find an interest outside the club, such as a wife. He likes you, he told me so, and frankly I thought he would, that is why I chose you for the post I advertised out of the host of applicants. I had already formed a plan, what do you think I want a paid companion here for? There's nothing to do except drive the car and that was really an excuse, my son quite often had a taxi anyway. Except for the fact that my late husband's car was standing idle in the garage I would not have advertised for someone to drive it anyway.'

Janet did not know how to reply to this outburst, it had to come anyway, she had known. She felt that something might be suggested by Jack if she could only have time to talk about things. 'I am going out and cannot stop to talk about things now,' she managed to stammer out, and hastily ran up the stairs to her room, it was the only refuge she had. After a short time she dressed carefully, stole out of the house and went to collect the Captain as usual. He was a little unsteady and not too coherent. He tried to say how nice she looked as she helped him up the stairs to his room to sleep it off. Then she very thankfully made her way to the garage where Jack was waiting to take her to his home.

His eyes shone as he greeted her and said how nice she looked. 'Mother will love you I know,' he announced. 'I have told her about you and that you lost your own mother.'

'I have something very important to discuss with you,' said Janet, and started to tell him how the situation had developed recently at the Kinder household. 'Frankly I shall have the sack if I don't agree to marry the Captain.'

Jack was astounded at this revelation. 'Surely you are mistaken, no one would hold a pistol at anyone's head like that.'

'Oh yes she would, she has, and she means it. He is a decent enough man if he would only stop drinking, he almost lives at that club. There are girls who might jump at the chance, of course he is a lot older than I am.'

'You are not in earnest?' asked Jack. 'Surely neither you or any other girl would contemplate marrying such a man just to keep a job?'

'You have a very romantic idea of women, I am very pleased that you have, I would not love you otherwise, I hope, that is if I had any say in the matter. It seems to me that you have a lot to learn about women. I met a wife once who was delighted to tell me that she always knew when her husband had been unfaithful because he brought her a present.'

Jack looked at her disbelievingly. 'I can't think any man would be so silly, let alone give himself away like that. What did she say to him in return?'

'Nothing, she knew that he would do it again and did not really mind as long as she had a nice home and enough money to bring her children up well, buy herself clothes and generally have a good life.'

'I can't understand any woman being satisfied to live such a life. She could not love her husband.'

'I expect she loved him once, although I believe, as I said, that some women marry for a home, for money, and for a good time. Haven't you heard of sugar daddies?'

They both burst out laughing at this, then Janet brought sanity back by saying, 'It's all very well to talk but if I lose my job I shall have nowhere to live, you forget.'

'I must admit I hadn't thought of that.'

'Well, now you know, if I don't give up my friendship with you I shall have nowhere to live.'

By this time they had arrived at a pretty garden gate with a rose covered archway over it. Jack opened the gate and ushered his guest rather proudly along the garden path and into the rose covered cottage. A rather plainly dressed, rosy-cheeked elderly lady, who walked with some difficulty, greeted them. 'Come along in, I am so glad to meet you, Jack has told me a lot about you, take off your coat, the tea is ready.'

She went before them into a little parlour with a round table in the centre with plates laden with scones, cakes and bread and butter. It all looked so welcoming and so homely that Janet felt the tears welling.

'How lovely,' she said, 'I never really had much home life, my own mother died whilst I was at school and I had to find myself a job very early in life. My father has married again and really there's no room there for me, but never mind about all that, the tea looks delicious, how lucky Jack is to have you.'

Mrs Willard looked pleased at this remark and started out of the room saying, 'It is I that is lucky to have him.'

Jack took Janet's coat and seated her where she could look out of the window. Clematis and roses vied for position around the window and an apple tree nearby looked likely to have a good crop of fruit. Over tea the three discussed Janet's position. 'You poor thing,' said Mrs Willard, 'You must get yourself another job, obviously you can't stay there.'

'I agree, but it's not so easy, you see I have nowhere else to live.'

'Can't you go home to your father whilst you look for something?' said the old lady.

'His wife does not make me welcome there, she has a family of her own and I would hate to force myself on her when I know I would not be welcome.'

'I admire you for that,' said Mrs Willard. 'But what are you going to do?'

'That is the trouble, I don't suppose I would have considered my present job if it had not offered a home as well.'

'She can't turn you out into the night.'

'I'll watch that,' put in Jack. 'She hadn't better.'

'I shall try for a post from the same source that I got that one, it was advertised in a magazine.'

Jack was very quiet for a while then suddenly he put down the cup he had been holding, deep in thought for some little time. 'I have an idea, you could get a job at the garage, just temporarily I mean, and live here, couldn't she Mother? We have a spare room.'

'I suppose she could for a while, just until she found somewhere.'

'You seem to have it all fixed up,' said Janet, very much touched by their kindness. 'What's this about a job at the garage?'

'Oh, it would not be a very grand job, but we could do with someone to do the booking, answer the telephone and perhaps serve a drop of petrol occasionally, it's a bit of a nuisance sometimes when my boss is away at one of the other places, there are five altogether you know, and I am perhaps up the road demonstrating a car. Someone calls for a drop of petrol, we don't sell very much, sometimes we go all day without selling a drop, there's that up-to-date filling station up the road. It isn't worth keeping a boy just for that job, whoever is handy mans the pump when required. Repairs and car supply are our main job really.'

'That sounds wonderful, I can drive too you know.'

'Yes, that could be very useful, sometimes we have to tow a car in or fetch one that a hirer has left somewhere. A few weeks ago I had to go to Scotland to fetch a car of ours that a customer had hired and no longer wanted so left it there.'

Suddenly the old lady, who had been very quiet, chipped in saying, 'They will have to give you a month's notice you know.'

Jack looked thoughtful. 'I should think it would be mightily unpleasant working out a month's notice there, would you like me to speak to the boss about a job there?'

Janet felt that things were going a little too fast for her. 'I suppose so, I don't have to take the job anyway without consideration.'

'I think I could almost say the job is yours,' put in Jack. 'Come on upstairs and see how you would like the bedroom.'

'That's just like my son,' said Mrs Willard. 'The job is settled before you begin in his eyes.'

Janet followed Jack up the cottage staircase and along a narrow passage, well-carpeted landing and into another room. It was small but looked as if it could be made very comfortable.

Looking out of the window there was a view over the houses to fields as far as the eye could see. 'How beautiful!' exclaimed Janet.

Jack came forward, his face alight with happiness and took her in his arms. 'Let's get married,' he said. 'What about it? Say yes.'

'You are in a hurry,' said Janet. 'We scarcely know each other.'

'I know you well enough, you are sweet, clean-living and have had a hard time. I am sure we could be happy with Mother in her cottage, she would not get in the way and you could do as you like, make a few changes perhaps.'

'Oh I could never do that,' said Janet returning his kisses. 'It's her house and I would be an intruder.'

'Well then, let's get married and live somewhere else.' He took her in his arms and covered her face with kisses. 'You are lovely you know, I have never met anyone I could love like you.'

'What about all those girls at the dance?'

'They meant nothing to me,' said Jack.

'They were keen enough to dance with you.'

'I don't even like them let alone want to marry them, let's talk it over with Mother, she is very sensible and will advise us what to do.'

After a long lingering kiss they went down to Mrs Willard who was in the kitchen. She seemed quite happy at the idea that Janet should come to live at the cottage for a while and said straight away, 'You can move in as soon as Jack can get the car ready.'

'What shall I pay you for the room?'

'Oh, we can settle that when you are ready to come, I am not a selfish person and have enough for my needs. I shall be glad of the company.'

The rest of the evening was spent in the little parlour together. Mrs Willard retired early and left them together. When eventually Jack accompanied her back to the Kinder home Janet felt happy in the thought that she had found a friend as well as a sweetheart, had somewhere to go and perhaps a job as well. As they were saying their last good night, Janet said, 'Yes, I will marry you.' She went into the house on a cloud.

Next morning the house was quiet as usual. The only sound was from Winnie, busy in the kitchen peeling potatoes or preparing the Captain's breakfast, sometimes humming to herself quietly. Janet made herself some toast and sat down at the kitchen table to look at the morning paper which had just arrived before Winnie took it upstairs. Janet's mind kept going round and round the subject of how she could give notice to leave the post. Should she give formal notice or should she acquaint Mrs Kinder of her wishes? The time came to get the car ready to take the Captain to his club. Janet brought the car round to the door and sat quietly waiting. Anything, she realized, to avoid meeting Mrs Kinder until it became inevitable. Should she tell the Captain? It would depend on his mood.

As it happened, when the Captain appeared he looked less worried than usual. He's in a good mood, thought Janet. 'Hallo, my dear, how are you?' He got into the front seat next to Janet.

'I am engaged to be married,' she stated.

'Oh, who to?'

'A young man named Jack Willard,' replied Janet, already half regretting blurting the news out like that.

'Isn't that the chap at the garage up the road? Where's the ring? I suppose he could afford to buy you one? His sort usually spend it all on beer and cigarettes, and girls I suppose,' he added as an afterthought.

Janet tried to hide her resentment and could not help feeling somewhat amused at the reception she had got from imparting the news. 'I haven't got the ring yet,' she replied. 'I only agreed last night.'

'Oh well, we shall be losing you then I suppose. Where are you going to live?'

'At his mother's.'

'Does she know?'

'Not yet, I shall tell her today.'

'Best of luck anyway, I don't blame you, it's not much of a life for a pretty girl like you here. I am not a marrying man myself as you know.'

He started to ramble on somewhat incoherently about life at sea and girls in other ports. Janet could not understand what he was talking about and was pleased when they arrived at the club.

'Same time as usual after lunch,' he said as he got out of the car. 'You will still be with us I suppose?'

Janet took this as a feeble kind of joke and drove away smiling.

She still felt the glow of happiness that she had acquired last night. She was, however, dreading the coming interview with Mrs Kinder and wondered if she should broach the subject over lunch.

The decision was taken out of her hands. Scarcely had she taken her seat at the table when Mrs Kinder asked, 'What time did you get in last night?'

'Oh, quite late, and I have some news for you.'

As soon as she had voiced the fatal words she realized that she should have waited until she had a ring on her finger to substantiate her announcement. However, she had now gone too far to retreat and continued, 'I am engaged to be married.'

Mrs Kinder opened her eyes very wide and said, 'You don't waste much time, who is the lucky man?'

'You would not know him, he runs the garage along the road.'

There was a pregnant pause for what seemed like an age. Both Madame and Mrs Kinder stared at the girl who sat motionless and silent.

'I don't believe you, if you think this is a joke it is a mean kind of joke. I must admit I thought you a decent respectable kind of girl, not one who would throw herself at any man that came along, I hope it is not a case of having to get married. I am glad my son is well out of this. You have let me down badly, I never suspected that you were the kind of girl that could use a situation to try to tie responsibility to some man, apparently any man who happens to be available. I suppose you got yourself into trouble and came here looking for a chance to latch on to any man you could find. I suppose my son was your first choice. Thank goodness he had too much sense to be taken in by you.'

Mrs Kinder was forced to stop for breath. Madame was sitting silent and staring blindly ahead. Janet immediately took advantage of the pause, 'It's not what you think,' she broke in, 'Jack and I met at the garage when I had to call with the car, we both fell in love and I think I am trying to be honest, telling you immediately. I could have continued here, letting you think I cared for the Captain for a long time, that is why I have tried to be honest, that is why I have told you at once, we only decided last night to become engaged.'

'All right, all right,' burst in Mrs Kinder, she had now regained her breath. 'You realize you can't stay here, I will advertise at once for a replacement, in the meantime you can drive the car and carry out your usual duties but you will eat in the kitchen with the maid.' Then a thought seemed to occur to her. 'Don't tell me that she is in this with you?'

'I don't know what you meant about Winnie, but I can tell you that she knows nothing about my affairs, also I can say that you are exceedingly lucky to have such a staunch and loyal employee working for you, it is more than you deserve. The end of my second month is due in a week's time and my salary is due then, I will leave then if you agree, or would you rather give me a month's notice as agreed on either side in the first place?'

'Oh leave when you like,' growled the lady and stormed out of the room.

Madame, who had been standing by silently whilst the altercation proceeded seemed to suddenly wake up. 'You are a silly girl you know, you could have had a good home here and a good and wealthy husband. He would never have been any bother, if my idea is right he won't be here for much longer, he's too fond of the old whiskey bottle. If you had played your cards right you could have ended up with the lot, I only wish I could have had the chance when I was your age.'

'I don't mean to be rude to you,' said Janet, 'but I would be glad if you would mind your own business.'

With this remark Janet left the room, she could not possibly have eaten anything, her appetite had completely deserted her. She went to her bedroom and sat down to collect her thoughts. She must somehow manage to carry out her usual duties calmly to the end of the month, in the meantime perhaps Jack would secure a post for her at the garage. She was quite excited at the prospect of working in the public eye, life would take on a different dimension, but best of all she was looking forward to being a wife. The wife of a handsome, strong and loving husband. Each time she thought of Jack she felt a great excitement, how lucky she was to have found such a handsome fellow, and how lucky she was that he loved her. Her mind drifted on to the day when she would again make wedding vows, then suddenly came the realization that she was not a single girl, she was a widow. How could she now tell Jack this well-kept secret? He would be shocked. She could not tell him.

Suddenly this spectre loomed up to haunt her. Why didn't she tell him in the first place? She had been afraid that the manner of her husband's death would come to light. She had killed him. Again all the horror of those first few weeks came back to haunt her. She had grown used to thinking it all past and forgotten. She could not risk losing the love and respect of Jack now. What would she do without him? Life had been almost a nightmare since she had left Scotland. Was that terrible episode to haunt her for the rest of her life? She must try to put it behind her, then a thought came to her like a flash of lightning. What about the marriage certificate!! It would have to be truthfully completed, what would the penalty be if she failed to declare that she was a widow. She tried to convince herself that it would not make any difference anyway. She must put off any idea of a wedding until she could think of a solution or manage to tell Jack her secret.

12

'Jack,' said his mother that evening, 'are you happy about this engagement to this girl?'

'Not "this girl" Mother, please call her Janet, you like her don't you?'

'Yes dear, she is a nice enough girl, and has had a sad experience it seems, are you sure that she is as innocent as she appears to be?'

'What do you mean Mother? Of course she is innocent.'

'It seems to me that there is rather indecent haste to get married.'

Jack burst out laughing. 'Oh Mother, you are old-fashioned, as far as I am concerned Janet is as pure as the driven snow.'

'As far as you are concerned, yes I can believe that, but what do you know about her life before you met her?'

'Of course I don't know all about her whole life, only that she had a job with this farmer and his son before she came to the Kinder household. She was very frank about that, he did try to kiss her or something, she was very frank about that too, that is why she came to work at the Kinder household, to get away from him.'

'It all sounds very strange to me, but I hope you will both be very happy, it won't be my fault if you aren't.'

Janet dreamed about a happy marriage with Jack that night. She dreamed that he was sleeping beside her. They had just made love. She had a feeling of dissatisfaction. She realized that her natural womanly inclination to hold back was not true to her natural instincts. She needed something loving and warm, some kind of foreplay, that was what she thought it was called. This instinct seemed to be sadly lacking in men. For instance their kisses were casual, bestowed like casual caresses, at least those she had accepted in her past experience with men. Perhaps I am different to other women, I have never felt any satisfaction from sex, only disappointment. It starts with kisses. Jack and I have got so far. Then with stroking and caresses. I begin to feel warm and happy, then a certain impatience seems to take possession of the man, are all men so impatient? Do they all want to get the sex act over as soon as possible? Men don't seem to realize that a woman's sex drive is just as strong and demanding as theirs, the difference being, it seems that with women there has to be love. With men it does not seem to matter about that, just attraction will be sufficient. Also, with women it builds up gradually. It seems to me that a woman who loves a man has two choices. She can experience quick and casual sex, as and when the urge takes her lover, leaving her aroused and dissatisfied and settle for that to keep her man happy, or she can delay and enjoy love, kisses and caresses, fending off any further culmination and run the risk of either being called a tease, or a woman that is never satisfied, or worse still, a woman that it is not possible for any man to satisfy. One hears of marriage guidance. One wonders if marriage guidance for men is really required, or are the natural instincts and desires felt by men impossible to hold in check and use with patience.

Janet awoke with a start. Had she been dreaming or was her brain working in some way to warn her against a hasty marriage? She knew that she loved Jack and she also now knew that she had never loved before. She was anxious to do nothing to spoil their chances of happiness. Somehow today she had to make some kind of decision and form a plan. After all, she had nowhere else to live at the moment but the Kinder's home. She could scarcely expect Jack's mother to take her in immediately.

Janet rose and breakfasted with Winnie in the kitchen telling her the news. 'Oh, I am sorry you are leaving,' said the girl. 'Is it the Captain? We got on so well.'

'Not exactly,' Janet replied, 'I hope I have a job at the garage to go to soon.'

'Where will you live until then?' asked Winnie. 'You can share my bedroom if you like until you get somewhere if Mrs Kinder turns you out.'

Janet was very touched at this spontaneous offer from the worried looking childish girl. 'I shall be all right Winnie, but thank you all the same, you are a true friend.'

Janet got the car ready as usual for the Captain and when he appeared he got into the front seat and said, 'I want to talk to you.'

'There really is nothing to talk about,' replied Janet.

'Why are you leaving us? Don't you like the job? You can have an increase in salary, I am sure, if you will change your mind.'

'That's very kind of you, and I really do appreciate it, however, I do not think this is a suitable post for me and anyway your mother has taken a dislike to me.'

'Has she by Jove, I thought she was very pleased with you, she said so to me some time ago. I suppose I shall have to put up with taxis again if you really can't stand the job.'

Janet felt unwilling to discuss the affair any further with the Captain and after she had left him at the club she called round by the garage to see if Jack had any news for her. He came out and sat in the car with her.

'I have some good news for you, at least I hope it is good news. You can start at the garage next week. You can start as a clerk but actually you will be asked to make yourself useful in any other way that is required. Answer the phone, copy out job sheets, make up bills, take cash, serve petrol if there is no one else handy, and take your turn on Sunday mornings to come in early and attend to the hire car customers who often collect cars early on Sunday for a day out. You will soon pick up what to do. What do you think about the job? Would you like it?'

'I think so, in any case I have to leave the Kinders in a week's time and have nowhere else to go. I have to get somewhere to live too, you know.'

'Yes dear, I know that and I have had a chat with Mother, we have plenty of room in our house, it's just that Mother likes the kitchen to herself and I don't think she would be too happy having to cook for three, I will try to talk her round. When do you think you would like to come over to talk to her about it?'

'Today if you like,' replied Janet. 'I don't want to cause her any inconvenience and extra work, I would help her and make it easier for her actually, I would have thought.'

'That is not exactly what worries her, she likes to do what she likes when she likes and has got used to having the house to herself. She is not as well as she would like us to believe, she suffers a lot with her legs I know, she has often left a cold meal for me and once or twice she stayed in bed for several days and would not see a doctor.'

'I see,' said Janet, 'will you be seeing her at midday?'

'Yes, I shall go home.'

'Will you say that I will be round to see her about three o'clock then?'

'All right, will you call at the garage first?' said Jack.

'Does your boss, what's his name?'

'His name is George Fuller.'

'Does he want to see me?'

'I don't think it matters, I have told him all about you, he is not often here anyway but he says that he thinks he's seen you. shall I tell you what he said?' asked Jack with a laugh.

'Oh, yes please.'

'He said, "Do you mean that handsome, dark-haired, long-legged piece that drives that old Navy block about"?' They both laughed heartily.

'I will call at the cottage then,' said Janet and drove away. She took the car back to the Kinder home and prepared to endure a trying hour at the table for lunch with Mrs Kinder and Madame. I shall be so glad when this is over, she thought, then remembered that Mrs Kinder had said that she was to eat in the kitchen with the maid. She looked in the dining room, having first ascertained that it was not occupied, to see that Winnie had laid three places as usual at the dining table. Going to the kitchen she found the maid busy cooking.

'Are you sure that I am to eat in the dining room?' she asked.

'Why ever not Miss?'

'I thought I was to have my meals with you in future.'

'You don't want to take any notice of her, she often says things she doesn't mean, then forgets all about them, you might be surprised to hear that she has given me a month's notice at least three times over the three years I have been here, and I have given her a week's notice several times. We both know it doesn't mean anything and I have just gone on as usual. You want to do the same.'

'Oh, she means it all right with me,' Janet replied. 'You see, I think she hoped that the Captain would fall in love with me.'

'That's a laugh,' said Winnie. 'He don't want to marry anybody, stop his little tricks it would. He gets blind drunk every night you know, the taxi driver knows him and helps to get him upstairs. That's why Mrs Kinder stays up so late. That's why your bedroom is right at the other end of the house.'

'I half expected that,' said Janet. 'Anyway, I shall know by tonight if I have anywhere else to go, and, I have another job.'

'What sort of a job is it if you don't mind telling me?'

'I don't mind at all, it is in the office at the garage and I think I have got it if I can find somewhere to live.'

They heard the ladies go into the dining room and soon Mrs Kinder gave her usual loud bang at the brass dinner gong. Janet walked into the room and took her usual place at the table. No comment was made by either lady and silence prevailed throughout the meal.

Janet dressed with care in her navy suit and spotless white blouse and went to call on Jack's mother. The old lady came primly to the door and ushered her into a cosy looking room with a small log fire burning although the day was warm still. It was barely autumn and Janet was rather surprised to see the fire. 'Sit down,' said the old lady, 'I don't usually light the fire so early in the autumn but I have got a bit of a chill and I do feel the cold these days, also I can air the clothes I have just been ironing in the kitchen.'

'Of course I understand, perhaps I shall be able to help you with some of the work if I come to stay here. Jack tells me that you are not too keen to have a lodger, or shall we call it a paying guest?'

'Call it what you like,' said the old lady rather sourly. 'It means that I shall have to share my home with a stranger.'

'Not with a stranger I hope,' said Janet. She could see that it was not going to be an easy task talking the old lady into letting her come to live at the cottage. Then she had a brainwave. 'I tell you what we could do, will you show me the bedroom you thought of letting me have?'

She followed Mrs Willard up the narrow stairs into the room at the back of the house. 'This is it, my son says he can put a small electric fire in it for you and there are already several places to plug in a light. You can use the kitchen, I suppose, to wash any clothes and share our sitting room evenings.'

'Oh, I have a much better idea than that now I have seen the room,' began Janet. 'I could have the room fixed up as a bed-sitting room, have a television set of my own, a fire, and could also do what small amount of cooking I need there, such as make toast. I could even have a little oven in the room, it would all be electrical and if we liked we could have a meter fixed up and then I could pay separately for what I use.'

The old lady listened carefully, nodding her head and looking thoughtful. 'Come on downstairs, I will make a cup of tea and we can talk about it.'

They went down to the cosy sitting room and a small tray soon appeared with an old-fashioned brown teapot with a hand-knitted cosy.

'I think we shall get on fine, once you have got used to the idea,' ventured Janet. 'I have never had a real home. My mother died when I was quite young and my father married again.'

'I am sorry to hear that, my husband died four years ago. Jack was born very late in life, I didn't marry until I was over forty, it has not been easy bringing Jack up but he is a good boy, I don't think he would bring any trouble home to me.'

'I'm sure he won't. What do you think of the bed-sitting room idea for me? And what about rent?'

'I shall have to leave that for Jack to work out, now that we have had a talk I don't feel so bad about it, I was dreading the thought that Jack might one day want to get married but I couldn't stand young children running about my home. It's all very worrying.'

'Not now, dear, I am sure,' replied Janet, sipping her weak tea from a china cup with roses on the side. 'I must go, and I am sure that Jack will be able to arrange things to the best advantage for you. I can let myself out. Goodbye for now.'

After dinner that evening Jack and Janet took a long walk and talked about the future, the job and the bed-sitting room. Jack was in favour of the latter, he said that there were times when his mother liked to snooze beside the fire in the afternoon and often in the evening. He knew that she did not much like the idea of having to share her sitting room. 'If we carry out the bed-sitting room idea I will be able to come and sit with you sometimes in the evening, and when we get married we can have that room as a sitting room and can share my bedroom, did you see it?'

'No I didn't, and don't be cheeky,' replied Janet, laughing, but a warm feeling of anticipation crept over her and she could feel a blush spreading over her face.

'You are a shy darling,' said Jack and moved to take her in

his arms.

'Not now,' she said. 'Let's go to the cottage and see what can be done about the room,' and they finished their discussion sitting on the somewhat hard old chairs in the old-fashioned bedroom that Jack was already picturing, after his handiwork and Janet's ingenuity had been brought to work. A microwave cooker, a fire, a neat table and some shelves for that corner, a chest and a cupboard. That was the list of requirements.

'There is a room hanging-cupboard outside on the landing,' said Jack. 'I am so glad that things have worked out like this, it will almost be as if we are already married.'

'Don't talk like that Jack, your mother will be shocked. We must have a clear understanding if I come to live here. We are not married and not living together either, we are friends, an engaged couple if you like, and until we are able to marry we must keep it that way. I would hate to cause your mother any worry or to have her regret having me to stay here.'

'All right, all right, we will go at the first opportunity to see a friend of mine who has a second-hand furniture shop. Perhaps he will take the old bed and anything else you don't want, also he may have what you are looking for.'

'Yes, I think that is a good idea,' said Janet, 'but now we must go and have a talk with your mother to see if she agrees with these plans, don't forget it's her house.'

'She'll agree all right, she will be very glad when it's all arranged and settled, I am sure. She is getting on, you know, and it will be good for her to have another woman in the house.'

'What if she does not want another woman in the house?' said Janet teasingly.

'No fear of that when I have finished talking to her, she will be glad too when we get married, I am sure.'

'I don't know about that,' said Janet.

'I do, now what about going to see the vicar?'

'You are joking of course,' said Janet. Her whole being began to tremble and and she grew afraid that Jack would notice her confusion but if he did he was only too pleased that he had caused some reaction in this apparently cool and calm young lady. 'Let us get settled first, please Jack, or at least let me get started in the new job, after all I might not like the job, I might not be able to do the work. I have not had office training, you know.'

'Never mind about that, I am sure you will make a success

of the job, you can start next Monday if you like, we haven't got anyone and we shall be glad to have you.'

After another chat with Mrs Willard, who had coffee ready, they told her of their plans. She seemed to agree and looked rather relieved.

13

The bed-sitting room had been satisfactorily furnished, thanks to Dan, the second-hand man. Mrs Kinder had accepted the inevitable and it was Janet's last night at the house. She had packed her small supply of clothes and felt sorely tempted to creep up to the attic and to help herself to some of the elegant clothes in the trunk. Madame Susette was leaving the following day and Janet thought it was most unlikely that Mrs Kinder would visit the attic for a long time, if ever again. Her memory was very poor and it seemed unlikely that she herself would ever remember what was in the trunk anyway. She had filled her own small case with her own clothes and had arranged to borrow the car next day to take her things to the cottage.

If I go now and put some of the clothes into that suitcase I saw on top of the chest, I feel certain that neither the clothes nor the case would be missed. I could take it down tonight and put it in the car boot at the back. Winnie will help me to carry my large case down in the morning.

She waited no longer but stole up to the attic. The dress she had borrowed for the dance lay on the top, the dress that had almost cost her Jack's love. No, she told herself, I don't want that one, but she could not resist the elegant fur coat that came next, it did rather smell of moth balls but that would soon go off. Putting her goods on a chair she closed the trunk and went to reach down the case. Wiping off the dust she opened it and was astounded to see a small, velvet covered case inside. Hastily she lifted it out and pressed the spring. The lid shot open and there in a pale satin bed lay a beautiful double string of pearls.

Oh, I would love these, dare I take them? Who is to know where they went? They have obviously been lying there for ages, Mrs Kinder has forgotten all about them, she seemed surprised to find so many clothes in the trunk when she brought me up first, I am sure if it had not been for the prompting of Madame she would have forgotten she had anything up here at all and Madame is unlikely to come visiting again for a long time.

Hurriedly she placed the pearls together with the clothes in the case and hurried down the stairs and into her room with them. She planned to take them down to the car quite early in the morning before anyone else was up. She spent her last night at the Kinders' house dreaming of what a lovely life she would have with Jack but her joy was somewhat marred by the thought that she would have to tell him sometime that she was not a single girl but a widow. She decided to tell him right away, at the first opportunity, he was very much in love with her and soon he would begin to think that she did not wish to get married at all if she put off going to see the vicar as he had suggested too long.

'There is something I must tell you Jack.'

It was the following evening. All her possessions were installed in her new abode and tomorrow she was to start her new job.

'Well, is it very important?'

'Yes it is rather, I have decided that I can't marry you without tell you more about my past life.'

'You have some dark secret to impart, you mean?' said Jack jokingly, then looking at Janet's face he could see that she was very worried about something. They were sitting in her new bed-sitting room, tired after moving things around and putting things right and to Janet's satisfaction.

Suddenly she could stand the strain no longer and blurted out, 'I have been married before, it was very short, my husband had an accident and is dead.'

There was a prolonged silence, then Jack said, 'Well, I must say I am very surprised, you seem to have got a lot in in a very short time in your life, why on earth have you kept it a secret until now?'

'I didn't think you would want to marry a widow,' sobbed Janet.

'It doesn't look as if I have much choice, does it? Luckily we did not go to see the vicar when I first suggested it.'

Jack turned his back on her and disappeared quickly down the stairs. Janet managed somehow to get through the rest of the day.

Janet started her morning at her new job at the garage feeling unhappy and sad, although she was pleased that she had got her confession over. Jack had scarcely spoken to her and he was soon busy in the repair shop after he had explained what her work would consist of and saw that she was familiar with the office and anything else that she would be required to do.

She soon learned what her duties were and soon noticed also that she was not the only woman who found Jack attractive. Ladies would come with their cars and instead of coming to the reception office they would go looking for Jack to explain to him what they thought was wrong. Polite as always, Jack would drop his tools, wipe his hands and come out to bend over the car engine laughing and chatting to the owner. Janet would try to hide her dismay when the talk seemed so prolonged that she began to think that there could not possibly be so much wrong with the car to talk and laugh about. She managed to contain her feelings for some time, she so loved Jack and he had assumed the major position in her mind and indeed in her life, she could think of nothing but his perfection. His smile made her feel happy and excited, did it also make other girls feel that way?

Each night she reassured herself that he loved her and only her, but he seemed cold somehow since she had blurted out her secret. Then one day a very well-dressed lady appeared with a very fine car. She came to the office and asked if someone could look at her car.

'What do you think the trouble is?' asked Janet.

'I don't know, do I? Where is the man around the place? He is tall and very nice looking, he knows my car, I have not been in lately, I have been abroad but he is the only one I will trust with the Rolls.'

Janet looked at the car, it was really splendid, she thought. Just then Jack came out, wiping his hands, and a welcoming smile radiated his face.

'Hallo, here's my friend and saviour,' said the lady, running forward and taking Jack's hand, ignoring the black grease that he had failed to remove. Jack's face lit up and he had eyes for no one and nothing but the lady and the car. Walking forward together the two soon had their heads together under the bonnet of the huge and splendid car.

Janet felt first of all anger, then rage. Somehow she managed to walk back into the office and tried to stop herself watching the pair through the window. Suddenly they both got into the car and Jack drove it out of the garage and off along the road. Janet managed to control her feelings with difficulty. Tears were welling up at the back of her eyes. They are friends. He knew her before he met me, she is rich and very beautiful, she will take him away from me. The thought kept worrying her mind. She is not a widow, she is not a widow.

I must stop this awful worrying, I must try to act naturally. After all, she is a customer, she has to be treated well, she obviously has money and is a good client. By the time the car arrived back on the garage forecourt Janet had composed herself enough to appear normal. The lady drove away. Jack came into the office and looked at the repair bookings.

'You will have to telephone this client and let him know that we are not able to take his car in on Wednesday after all,' he said.

'Why?' asked Janet. She knew what the reply would be.

'Because we will be working on the Rolls for at least two days.'

Janet could not stop herself, she said, 'So you are going to put that woman before our regular clients?'

Jack looked rather hard at her and said, 'Any objections?'

Janet saw a look on Jack's face that was not familiar to her. She felt her face colouring up and before she could think she said, 'Because she is a pretty woman and a friend of yours I suppose. I saw the way she looked at you and the way you smiled back, you had eyes for no one else as soon as she came on to the forecourt. I didn't exist as far as you were concerned, you just got into the car beside her and drove off completely ignoring me.'

Jack looked at her in astonishment. 'She is a very wealthy lady, with a very lovely car and we are honoured that she brings it here, she could easily have taken it to a rival firm but she trusts me and knows she will get a good job done here.'

'And a bit of attention and flattery as well, I suppose,'

Jack's eyes flashed. 'Don't be ridiculous, I don't have to come and ask you if you approve, in any case she wouldn't be interested in a garage mechanic.'

Janet's temper rose at this last jibe. 'She looks to me as if she wouldn't care who and what it was as long as it was male and she could buy his attention with money, of which she looks as if she has plenty.'

Immediately Janet had shouted these words she would have

given all she had to get the words back. The look that Jack gave her was one she had never seen on his face. Jack turned on his heel and walked away, into the rear of the garage, Janet fought to keep the tears of hurt and frustration away. The telephone rang and brought some kind of order to her frantic mind. She took the message and wrote it down. Now that the schedule of work had to be changed owing to the Rolls Royce job she couldn't say when this client's job could be fitted in. She said that she would ring back and wrote down the message. I suppose I should go and ask one of the men, or ask Jack, she thought. I can't go into the workshop with a red face like this. As she wrote a car appeared and a driver started to help himself to petrol. Having filled his tank he came forward to pay.

'Are you all right dear?' he asked in a fatherly way. 'You look as if you had been crying.'

'Yes, thank you, I had a fly in my eye but it is all right now.'

'You have to be careful with the eyes you know, they are very fragile.'

'Yes, I know,' said Janet. 'It is kind of you to ask.'

'Boss away?' asked the man. 'You shouldn't be here on your own, some funny people about these days.'

'Oh no, the men are at work inside, thank you all the same for your kind thought.'

Somehow these few kind words had cheered her up and she was now beginning to realize how silly she had been, letting her feelings get the better of her in such a childish way. She decided at once to try to put things right and started to walk through the garage looking for Jack, finally she located him with his head hidden under the bonnet of a large car. As she came and stood beside him he took no notice of her and continued to work.

'May I speak to you?' she said.

'Not now, I am busy.'

'Too busy to listen to something that is important to me and I think to you?'

'I don't get paid for listening, I have more important work to do if I want to get this job finished.'

Janet felt hot waves of colour cross her face. 'Finished in time to start on that fancy woman's job I suppose,' she flashed back.

Turning on her heel she rushed back to the office, put on her coat and started walking off along the road in the opposite direction to home.

As she walked her temper cooled. I am being very silly, suppose someone walks into the office. No one would see them, they could go off with the money or anything else. No one knows that I am away, I am being silly and childish. I must go back. She kept walking and thinking to herself, I must go back. Then full realization suddenly came to her. I must be mad, I shall lose the job, I am not reliable. I must get used to seeing Jack talking nicely to lady customers. They are our bread and butter.

Suddenly she turned and hurried back up the road. All this is because I kept my previous marriage a secret from him. He is so annoyed with me he is thinking twice about keeping our engagement. After all he has not yet given me a ring. I must at all costs keep my job at the garage, at least for the present, I have nowhere else to go. Just as she came within sight of the forecourt a car drew into it and the driver started to help himself to petrol. She hurried along the road and walked into the office. There stood Jack.

'So, you have decided to come back have you? I saw you go. Now perhaps we can get on with some work.'

He walked out of the office and back into the garage as the customer came to pay for his petrol.

'It's nice to have a polite young lady here now, I shall know where to come in future when I want any service,' he said.

The rest of the day was uneventful and soon it was closing time, Jack and Janet went home in silence and not a word was spoken throughout the evening. Janet's thoughts hovered between the feeling that she would give anything to have things back on their old footing, and feeling angry and frustrated that she could do nothing about Jack's popularity with good-looking and rich lady clients. She kept reassuring herself that he had chosen her from all others, then reminding herself that he had not known that she had been married before and was deceiving him.

Why did I not realize what I was letting myself in for? Perhaps I should look for a job somewhere else, no, that would be worse, I should never see him again then. How silly I am, if only he would speak to me, would reassure me.

Bedtime came and they both retired without a word. Mrs Willard had retired early saying that she felt in pain with her legs. Janet lay thinking and wondering if Jack was still awake, perhaps she could get him to talk and bring to an end this silly quarrel. She got up and stole gently along the corridor and listened outside his door. Suddenly a loud snore broke the silence.

'He doesn't care, he can sleep soundly in spite of my misery. I can't stand this.

She went downstairs and made herself a cup of tea, she sat drinking it and thinking to herself.

I seem to have got myself into a stupid mess and I don't know how to get out of it. Suppose I start to smile and try to be friendly with some of the men who come to the garage, instead of remaining just polite and perhaps rather discouraging? Perhaps Jack would be annoyed, no, I expect he would be pleased. I can't win, it was silly of me to think he only had eyes for me. I'm so unhappy, what can I do? Perhaps I can go back to the Kinders, no, they wouldn't have me.

Next morning the two were away from the house early. They had heard nothing of Jack's mother but this often happened. The morning passed quickly and Jack announced at midday that he was going home for something he had forgotten and would be back to share the packed lunch they usually took together. Janet was making the coffee in the office when she saw Jack drive up and jump out of the car in great haste.

'I can't wake mother up,' he said. 'She didn't get up, she's still in bed and looks as if she's dead.'

'Have you sent for the doctor?' asked Janet.

'No, we'll do that now.'

* * *

Mrs Willard had passed away in the night and the doctor could find no cause of death. 'There will have to be an inquest,' he said. Janet felt that there was something terrible at work again. She remembered the horror and foreboding she had felt when her baby was found dead. She consoled herself somewhat thinking that she was not known here and all her past was gone and forgotten anyway. Jack would have been shocked and quite horrified if he had known about that too.

The garage was closed on the day of the inquest. Many questions were asked. Jack first of all gave his account of how they had not disturbed his mother early as they often went to work leaving her to sleep as long as she wished. The doctor reported that a post mortem had revealed that death was caused by an overdose of drugs. What was the last evening drink his mother had taken? Jack was asked.

'I usually take her a cup of milk or some such thing up to Mother. She retires early and I don't disturb her but leave it on her table beside the bed.'

Janet was called next. She said that she had made a cup of Horlicks when she retired and had taken it into the old lady who had asked for it to be left on the bedside table to cool.

'Did you get on well with her?' she was asked.

'Yes, quite well,' she replied.

The result was that no satisfactory answer seemed to have been reached, except that Janet was under suspicion and was kept overnight for further questioning. Next day she was informed that she was suspected of murder and would have to remain to await trial.

The day of the trial finally arrived and Jack was put into the witness box and looked across at Janet. He had not been allowed to see her but had written a note. He told of all his love and loyalty. He said that he knew she was innocent and was waiting for her when she was released. Janet treasured the note and had kept it near all the time. She looked across at Jack in the dock with her soul in her eyes. She expected that all her short past life would be revealed. The death of her baby would come to light and that would sound like an unsolved crime. She felt sure that fate was weighted against her and almost gave up hope entirely.

Why do I want to live anyway? she asked herself. I have no one to turn to. No friends. My father never wants to see me again, when he hears of this he will feel justified.

'Did you hate Mrs Willard?' came the question, Janet scarcely heard.

'No,' she replied at length.

'Was she kind to you?'

'Yes.'

'You have a father alive I believe?'

'Yes.'

Now the dreaded questions were coming.

'Has he remarried?'

'Yes.'

'You are a married woman?'

'Yes.'

Janet looked across at Jack. His face was stony. She could not tell what he thought.

'You had a child?'

'Yes.'

'It was found dead in its perambulator?'

'Yes. Yes, Yes,' she said. 'Take me out and lock me up, I am of no use to anybody.'

'Take her out,' came the word, and a wardress kindly led her away to await the verdict. Half an hour passed. Then the door opened and a white-faced Jack appeared.

'Come along darling, you are free.' He folded his arms around her and kissed her wildly. 'I love you, I love you. Never mind the past. I know you are innocent my darling, why didn't you tell me? How you must have suffered. You have nothing to be ashamed of. Come home to our cottage. I will take care of you.'

Then came the vital news. The lady librarian had just telephoned to say that in one of the library books that Mother had had, a note had been found, it was addressed to Doctor Stern and said that she had taken her own life. She knew that she would become a burden to her son and hoped with all her heart that he and Janet would live a happy life together in the cottage that she loved.

14

'Hello Mr and Mrs Jones, my name is Westlake, Tom Westlake, please call me Tom.'

Will and Annie Jones preceded the tall, good-looking visitor into their very comfortable, if rather old-fashioned lounge. Will indicated a seat and Tom Westlake seated himself. Opening his well-stocked briefcase he spread various coloured leaflets, all rather thumbed, on the table.

'You are both retired, I suppose,' said Tom.

'Are you wondering what to do with your savings? How much have you to invest, may I ask?'

'Steady on,' replied Will, 'we both have some savings which we mainly have invested in building societies, a friend pointed out to us that we could possibly get a much better return from your kind of investments. We don't know much about it really and it is very kind of you to make the journey to advise us. My wife is rather fixed in her ideas and always says that building societies are safe. One may not grow very rich but at least one is not likely to lose anything.'

Tom laughed. 'You certainly won't grow very rich that way, Mrs Jones. What interest are you getting now? About seven per cent, I venture to say.'

'I worked very hard and saved a long time to get the small amount I have,' said Annie.

'Please look at these figures, they represent the interest acquired over the last seven years, I call it interest but in this case it would be dividends, the same thing really as far as you are concerned, on money invested in one of our trusts. Of course I won't deceive you, dividends can go down as well as up but broadly speaking, profits have been, on an average, as you will see, well over ten per cent for a number of years. Of course we can make no promise. I can understand Mrs Jones how you feel and can recommend a reasonable safe investment for you. I feel that your husband would perhaps be prepared to go for something a little more profitable and I think I have just the thing for you, Mr Jones.'

The two picked up the various brightly coloured brochures and tried to study them. They tried to pretend that they could see what Tom was referring to but all the printed words and most of the figures were in a language that might as well have been Dutch or German to the old and somewhat poorly educated couple. This Tom seemed a very nice fellow, and what reason could he have to tell them anything that was not true? He didn't know that they could not understand what he was talking about, though the old fellow.

'How soon could you realize you capital, may I ask?'

'I have most of it invested in building societies too and it requires three months notice to obtain the cash without loosing three month's interest.'

'Don't worry about that,' replied Tom. 'What would you lose? about two pounds where with us it could make seven. Of course I make no promises, you understand.'

'Would you like a cup of tea?' asked Annie.

'Oh yes please,' replied Tom and Annie went out to put the kettle on.

Tom asked, 'What kind of business did you have before you retired?'

'We were in domestic service and we are not ashamed of it either.'

When Annie returned with the tea Tom said to her, 'I expect you are pleased to be a busy housewife for a change, I must say that it suits you. You look really charming handing round the tea. Oh, how I wish my wife was domesticated.'

Will did not know how to respond to this obvious flattery and said, 'She does her job as she always has'

Tom realized that he had perhaps overdone it to these simple people and quickly said, 'Now let's get down to business, how much would you like to invest? Shall we say £60,000 each for a start?' Then he proceeded to paint a very attractive picture of how it would grow and grow. 'Of course,' he said, 'if you decide to let it lie it could almost double itself in time, you know.'

Annie listened to all this talk and looked from time to time at her husband. She knew that he had been interested in the conversation of some of his friends lately. One had rather boasted about his gains and had hinted that he knew just what shares to buy. Annie trusted her husband entirely and although at times she thought he was almost too careful she knew that he was not likely to be tempted into any rash undertaking.

After a cup of tea and a little more light talk Tom Westlake suddenly looked at his watch and said, as if surprised, 'Oh dear, I must be going, I have another appointment to keep. Tell you what, I will call again in a couple of weeks' time, that will give you time to think things over and to draw out the cash you want to invest. Here is my home address but I am away a lot so perhaps you would like to make a firm date now?'

A date was made, rather reluctantly on the part of Will, and Annie took her visitor to the cottage door and waved him goodbye.

Will and Annie watched his departure almost afraid to meet each others eyes. 'What do you think?' asked Will. 'He seems a genuine sort of chap don't you think?'

'You know what I think,' replied Annie. 'He seems a bit too nice for my liking, however, that's his job, it wouldn't be any use for a firm to send a rude, impolite fellow to talk to people, we must give the whole thing careful thought though. As you know I am very much against taking unnecessary risks but it sounds as if good profits are to be made and with things going up all the time and our savings getting worth less and less we could do with a bit higher rate of interest, it's the loss of three months interest that annoys me.'

'Yes,' replied Will. 'That is aggravating but I don't think that he would mislead us, he did say that we could very soon recover that as the rate we would get would be so much higher.'

'I don't understand that, I must admit.'

Tom Westlake arrived home rather late that evening. He found his wife Elaine looking a little impatient, she had a nice meal waiting and served it immediately. Afterwards the couple relaxed and Tom started to say that he had a bright idea.

'If it's anything like other bright ideas you have had lately I would rather not hear about it.'

'No, this is a really good one and I feel sure we could work it together.'

'If I have got to do all the typing and stay at home all alone night after night whilst you chase after people to advertise in that silly magazine I am not interested,' replied Elaine.

'Is it my fault that I am only on commission?'

'Well, go on. It couldn't be worse than the job I have been doing today. What do you think that Mrs Natal that calls herself a friend asked me to do today? I had on that skirt I made and mistakenly told her that I had made it from a remnant. She said how clever I was with a needle and how lucky, and then asked me if I would like to do a little sewing job as she was hopeless with a needle. I said all right, trying to be friendly, and what do you think she produced? A pair of her husband's old trousers. She assured me that they had been cleaned but asked if I could make her little boy a pair out of the best part of them. I didn't know what to say. Then when I said I was busy she said, "Of course I would pay you". I just walked out of the house.'

'I should think so, what an insult. No, it's nothing like that. If we are careful we could acquire a great deal of money. How would you like to live on a beautiful South Sea island?'

'Don't talk such rot, I am not exactly an idiot you know, we have scarcely enough money to pay the rent and you talk of trying to save up to buy a house in the country where we could keep hens and live on nearly nothing.'

'Stop,' put in Tom quickly, 'this is different, in three weeks time I may be picking up a substantial sum that would be a start for us.'

'Well, if you have any money to spare I would like a new coat and we need some tea towels, I am tired of hemming round pieces of your old shirts to dry the plates on.'

'You should not dry the plates. I am always telling you that there is no need to dry them if you use plenty of hot water and two bowls. Rinse the dishes in the second bowl and they will drain themselves quite dry and clean.'

Elaine grew red in the face and it seemed that another of their noisy arguments were unavoidable. Tom recognized the signs, walked over and took his wife in his arms and kissed her on the lips.

'Come and sit down here and listen to me,' he said.

Elaine, looking surprised, pushed her chair back from the table and seated herself next to Tom on the large settee.

'Today,' started Tom, 'I called on a simple old couple, they are almost exactly like a lot of people I have recently come into contact with. As you know I work on commission and sometimes I have to make many calls with very little reward but just lately the newspapers are full of "get rich" advertisements. They print a table giving figures that show how people who have invested money in stocks and shares have doubled their investments in a very short time. This is usually followed by a sharp drop and often people lose a lot of money. However, at the present moment things do look very rosy and lots of people are feeling very dissatisfied with their building society interest and want to invest in something better. For instance, next month I have an appointment to see an elderly couple, the two I have seen today. I am sure that I shall come away from there with their life savings which they will give me to invest for them. Recently I have handed over cheques to the value of nearly a million pounds to the company. What is to prevent me from paying the money into my own bank next time?'

Elaine stared at her husband, scarcely able to believe what she heard. 'Do you mean steal it?' she stammered out at length. 'Have you gone out of your mind?'

'No I haven't, but I am sick of using my whole will-power and persuasive ability to make people decide to put their money, often their life savings, trustingly into the hands of some previously unknown people and being paid a measly pittance for doing so. I don't like what I have to do but I might just as well do it for my own benefit as for a boss who scarcely thanks me and who pays me, as I said, a measly pittance. He expects my loyalty and hard work and scarcely has the manners to thank me.'

'You are talking like this because you don't like your boss,' said Elaine. 'After all, it is a job, your car is supplied, otherwise we would not have a car, remember? And it would be awful to be unemployed again. Do stop talking like this, it's not like you, the man I admire and love. After all, we are much better off today than we were last year. I was just beginning to make some plans towards having a home of our own and perhaps starting a family.'

Elaine looked rather embarrassed and sent a sideways glance at Tom.

'If this idea I have could be carried through, with your co-operation, we could have a beautiful home. You would be able to lie in the sun all day and swim in our pool if you liked. We could be quite rich and you have to admit you love the sun. We could go to live in a country where the sun shines all the time.'

'Stop it, stop it,' broke in Elaine. 'It's all very well for you to assume yourself painting a wonderful picture like that but I am not exactly a fool, I know that some shady deal, or even some crime you want to plan is at the bottom of all this talk. I will tell you now, once and for all, I will have nothing to do with anything you plan to make us rich quickly. As you know, I am not fond of spending money and I have never grumbled at you or blamed you in any way for our present situation. Yes, I would love to have children but I am prepared to wait until we are able to bring them up well and live a reasonably good life.'

Elaine caught sight of the impatient look on Tom's face and stopped talking. She walked up to her husband and, putting her arms around his neck, she kissed him lingeringly on the mouth. Much to her surprise and dismay Tom pushed her impatiently away and said, 'It's all very well for you to preach, you have not even listened to my plan. It's not exactly easy but it could be carried out quite successfully. One needs to plan it well and one also needs the help of someone who can really be trusted.'

Tom's face mirrored his excitement and once again his voice rose as he paced the room, ignoring completely his wife and the food laid out on the dining table. Elaine walked into the kitchen. She felt deeply hurt at being repulsed so carelessly. She could not understand her husband's sudden excitement. Theirs had been a happy marriage so far although they had suffered through lack of employment. Tom had refused to take any job offered that he felt was beneath his capabilities. He was not unaware that he was well endowed with charm and when an old friend from college days had suddenly appeared and had introduced his father it had proved an exciting day for Tom.

Mr Law was the principal of a large firm of stockbrokers and after a chat he had recognized Tom's charming manner and subsequent potential, and had become very impressed. Soon he had occasion to flatter himself that he had made the right choice. Tom had seemed so delighted at the offer of a job that he had overlooked the small details, one of which was that his salary was infinitesimal and depended altogether on the amount of commission that Tom could earn in addition.

Tom had already proved that he could almost get blood out of a stone. Many times he had been sent to call on doubtful customers who had a long history of parsimony and had returned with a large cheque which was to be invested in some kind of stocks or shares with the company.

Mr Law was not slow in showing his pleasure and always made Tom feel excited and appreciated by handing out lots of flattery. For a start Tom had felt very happy that his skill and the results he achieved were not going unnoticed. Then, after a time, he began to think that it seemed a shame that he had to do it all for someone else. His share seemed so small compared with the large cheques he handed over regularly that had been placed in his hands smilingly and trustingly by his clients.

Suddenly today the thought had occurred to him, why not keep the money? Why not make a list of his most promising clients, arrange to delay payment for some and to try to advance payments from others in order that a very large sum would be put into his hands during a short period, perhaps one day? He could then cash all the cheques and gather the full amount, placing it in some foreign bank where it would be untraceable. Then, having everything planned and ready, he and Elaine could leave the country and start all over again in some beautiful sun-kissed land together. The plan would need a lot of organizing, also he would need the help and co-operation of someone he could absolutely trust. The most obvious one of course was Elaine, but Elaine had such scruples. He had always admired her for her high principles as well as her more obvious attractions, of course. Her obvious beauty. She was tall and well-proportioned. She had the gift of always appearing to be well-dressed at any gathering they had occasion to attend.

Tom had enough personal vanity to see that other men took notice of her and to feel pleased and proud. She had deep, auburn, luxurious hair, a ready smile and large, appealing eyes.

Tom had been hopelessly bowled over and had completely fallen to her charm. That was over three years ago and his efforts to provide for her in the manner to which she had been accustomed (she came from a wealthy family) had not exactly been successful. However, Elaine had been the first to admit that he had done his best and she had allowed her love and admiration to blind her somewhat to any faults he might have.

They ate their meals in silence and then Tom sat down with

a notebook in his lap working out figures whilst Elaine was busy in the tiny kitchen. When all was tidy she ventured back into the room and went to turn on the television. Tom immediately looked up from his notes and said harshly, 'Do we have to have that noise?'

'You usually enjoy this programme,' replied Elaine, turning it off. 'However, I have some needlework to do if you wish to work at your correspondence.'

'It's not correspondence,' replied Tom quite snappily. 'I am working out a plan to get rich quickly, the one you are not interested in, remember?'

Tom returned to his notebook whilst Elaine sat in silence. Suddenly she could stand it no longer. Smarting from the rebuff she had received when proffering a kiss, she suddenly rose from her chair and walked out of the room without a word and went into their one and only bedroom. She had often wished that they could live in a better neighbourhood and felt disinclined to invite her family and friends to this small suite of rooms they had found, convenient and fairly cheap as it was, and sufficient for their immediate needs.

Elaine had often thought of trying to get some kind of job for herself but she had no training and although well-educated and of good family her clothes were getting shabby and she felt self-conscious when talking to people. Her mother was dead and her father's house was ruled by a somewhat dragon-like housekeeper. She had often thought that perhaps her father would marry again but on the few occasions that she and Tom had happened to see him in a restaurant the lady he had been with had not seemed quite his type. That is to say, she had no resemblance in looks, manner or appearance to his first wife and Tom had once remarked, 'The old boy seems to be living it up a bit' or words to that effect. There had been no effort to introduce the lady in question and they had resolved to turn a blind eye in future when coming across a similar occasion.

Elaine had thoughts at times that she afterwards felt quite ashamed of. Was Tom disappointed that his father-in-law did not make any offer to help either of them, with money or with the offer of a job in any one of the various companies that he associated with? She privately thought that her father had labelled Tom as something of a 'Smart Alec'. This was a great pity really, as Tom's manner was largely assumed to hide his innate shyness and in the hope that those he met would be impressed. His manner had certainly worked with his present employers. He always assumed an air of confidence whatever the circumstances, they were encouraged and pleased with his efforts but seemed quite slow in offering much reward for the same.

Suddenly Elaine decided to try to agree with Tom and to try to help his plans and ideas. After all, she was his wife and he was entitled to expect loyalty and help from her of all people. She washed, changed into one of Tom's favourite dresses and went to find him. He sat at his desk with pen in hand, surrounded with travel books and pieces of paper. When Elaine stole quietly across the room in a way she often used to try to persuade him to 'leave it all' until tomorrow and to come and have a chat, he pushed away the travel books and closed down the desk with a snap. Turning a tired and worried looking face around, he half expected harsh words to greet him. Instead a soft hand caressed his brow and a warm cheek was offered for a kiss.

'I know you are worried darling, and I will do my best to try to help you. Let me hear about this wonderful plan you have to make a fortune and to go to live in a lovely South Sea island.'

'It's not as straightforward as that, you know,' replied Tom. Turning around he pulled his wife on to his knee and kissed her hungrily. 'I do love you, you know. All my plans are to make you happy and comfortable. I know you long to have a child and there is nothing I would like better, but we must make for ourselves a better way of life first. Don't you agree?'

'Of course I do dear, and I am prepared to listen to your plans and to help you all I can if there is anything I can do.'

Tom laughed and looked still more worried. Then Elaine said, 'You realize that I can't ask Daddy for money if it is capital we need. I think I would rather do anything than ask him for anything.'

'Don't worry dear,' replied Tom hastily. 'If we could carry out my plan there would be no need to ask anyone for anything at all. I need someone I can really trust to help me and there is no one I would rather have than you.'

'Well dear, come and sit over here. I will get you a drink and you can tell me all about it.'

They made themselves comfortable on a large old settee and

Tom started to explain. 'I handle very large sums of money almost every day, you know. Some people I have to see are very rich. They make casual requests such as "Take this cheque for forty thousand pounds and invest it in some decent shares". Sometimes I feel quite sure that they have no real idea of what they are actually worth. Only the other day a fellow made an appointment to see me about an investment. He didn't actually ask for me as he had never met me, but the firm recommended me. He said that he had around fifty thousand pounds that he had to "do something with" saying that he had just been paid out from a deal he had made and he wanted to put it what he called "on ice". I suggested certain shares, he said he had heard that they were on the "up and up". When I got back to the office I found that he had already invested over a hundred thousand in the same company and I feel sure that he had forgotten all about it. Also the silly man had made the cheque out to me personally. How silly can you get. It doesn't seem fair that one man should have so much money when others, like ourselves, have to work so hard for a mere pittance.'

Elaine listened and felt that she could understand how Tom felt, but she was very frightened at the idea that some of the money might be diverted into Tom's pocket. She could guess that all this talk was leading up to some plan to turn some of the money in his direction. She decided to listen in silence to all he had to say.

Tom very quickly warmed to his subject and said that he could make plans to obtain a very large sum which they would need to make his project worthwhile. 'It might be some time before the right moment arrives,' he said. 'There are at least three clients I have to see in the near future who will have considerable sums to invest. I shall have to make a very quick decision when the right moment arrives, that is when I shall need your help. The thing is, can I rely on you? It is certain that I can't carry out the whole operation alone. What do you think?'

'I would like to hear more about the plan before I make any decision,' replied Elaine.

'I can't tell you all about it and then have you laugh in my face, then know that you will tell the whole story to somebody like some wonderful joke.'

Elaine held back any feelings of anger. She knew that she had to find out what this great plan was. She very much feared that

Tom was impetuous enough to get himself into very serious trouble. She assured him that she was keen to hear his plans and would help him all she could.

Tom continued to talk in glowing terms of his plan and to paint a mental picture of the glorious life they could live together in some lovely foreign land.

'I can easily arrange to collect a large sum of money. I see wealthy clients every day and some of them are just ignorant people who have no idea what to do with the money anyway. I promise you that if you will help me you will not regret it. I will not hurt anyone by borrowing any money from them if they really can't afford it.'

Elaine listened and noted that Tom refrained from using the words 'cannot afford to lose it'. She knew that he was planning something very wrong and could not think at present of any way to stop him. She thought that worry and lack of money had affected his reasoning. It must be difficult, she thought, when one is continually associating and talking to people who acquire money so easily and talk about it casually to keep a level head. It was obviously no use arguing with him or trying to dissuade him from carrying out his plan. I must appear to go along with all his plans for the present in order to find out just what is going on and then think of some way to stop him. She sat listening for a long time whilst Tom outlined his plans to gather together all the cash he could and then to adopt a different name and to leave the country.

He talked of depositing money in a Swiss bank. Elaine knew nothing about finance but this sounded like robbery, and noticing the strange glint in her husband's eyes and his already rather furtive manner, she became very worried. She continued to listen and tried as much as possible to encourage him to confide his plans.

'What about passports?' she asked.

'I can get ours changed to another name, I am sure. There are people who will do anything for money.' Elaine had difficulty in stopping herself from saying the words that came into her head, 'and you are one of them'. But she knew that the only way to stop him in this foolish and criminal plan was to appear to agree for the present in order to find out just what he had in his mind.

'It would be your job,' he said, 'to clean up all our belongings then. To remove all our belongings from the flat and to obliterate all traces of our occupation. Then to book our tickets in another name and to keep everything very strictly secret. It would be fatal if anyone at all had the slightest idea of what we plan or where we are going. Now, what do you think?' Tom looked appealingly at his wife. 'Will you go along with me? I promise you a wonderful time.'

Elaine could think of nothing else to say but 'Yes darling'. Then , trying to cheer him out of his present mood added, 'It was for better or for worse, dear.'

'It's not a joke,' answered Tom, 'it's a very serious and complicated plan and will need a lot of planning, not least of all your co-operation.'

'Father will want to know where I am,' put in Elaine suddenly.

Tom jumped up and glared at her saying, 'There you go, I guessed as much. I wish I had kept the whole thing to myself, there are plenty of girls who would be only too happy to co-operate, to help me and to share the wonderful life in a beautiful land.'

Elaine could see at once that she had said the wrong thing again and tried to placate Tom by saying, 'Of course I was only joking dear, come, let's go to bed. I really am tired and you look absolutely worn out.'

* * *

After a restless night Tom was rather late the following morning and hurried away with scarcely a word to his wife. He arrived at the office to find his secretary, whom he had previously scarcely noticed, looking very attractive. As she leaned over him with the correspondence of the morning he had a faint whiff of some kind of engaging perfume and looked up to meet a pair of very large dark eyes and a rather provocative expression. He had scarcely noticed the girl before but was feeling rather hurt at Elaine's lack of admiration of his wonderful plan, and without stopping to think he said, 'What are you doing tonight?'

Nancy was completely taken by surprised. She had admired Tom for some time but knew that he was married. She was not averse to a good time if an opportunity arose. She flashed him a meaningful look and said, 'Won't your wife wonder where you are?'

Tom was always a quick thinker, after all Elaine had not given him much praise for his wonderful plan. 'You could telephone her and say that I have to see a client.'

'All right, I will phone her right away, perhaps we could go to some quiet little place where the food is good. Shall I get your calls for tomorrow worked out?'

'You are very quick to respond,' replied Tom, and they got to work.

Nancy said that she would like to call in at her flat on the way as the left the office. 'You can come in and have a sherry whilst I change if you like. Perhaps you would run me home in your car and then we can go on from there.'

Tom agreed, privately thinking what a good sport she was.

Nancy's flat was really only a bed-sitting room with a tiny annexe for a kitchenette, but Tom felt very comfortable and welcome as he enjoyed his sherry and looked round the room. It seemed a bit cramped and after helping himself to a second sherry he began to contrast Nancy with Elaine, to Elaine's detriment.

'I am sure that this girl would jump at the chance to go abroad for good with me,' and then Tom suddenly told himself that such a thought was unthinkable.

When Nancy appeared she had donned a rather daring, colourful dress and looked quite provocative. They were shown to a quiet little table and Tom chose some attractive looking wine. As the time passed they each enjoyed more to drink than perhaps was wise. After all, Tom had to drive his car home. As they left the restaurant together Nancy rather hesitatingly suggested that Tom should stay at her place overnight if he liked.

'What?' started Tom. 'You have only got one room.'

'Nobody will know that if you don't tell them, will they?' replied Nancy.

'Well, I must admit I don't much like the idea of driving back tonight, but we will have to think of a good excuse, my wife will go crazy with worry if I don't turn up soon.'

'We can surely think of some excuse, can't you tell her that you are a bit under the weather and have been overworking and so have decided that it would be better to stay overnight in a hotel?'

'Well, I suppose I could. I hope that she believes me.'

'Why shouldn't she?' Surely you are not in the habit of lying to her.'

'Of course not. I can easily say that I don't feel well enough to tackle the drive and that I am going to a small place that I know. I will have to ring off quickly or she will want to know where it is.'

'If you use a phone box that won't be difficult,' laughed Nancy.

Tom put on his coat and went to find a phone box, feeling rather guilty. Settling himself comfortably on Nancy's settee Tom could not stop himself from bringing up the subject of rich people who were careless with their money and who, he thought, deserved to lose it. Nancy agreed and Tom felt more and more encouraged to talk and finally began to paint a picture of a wonderful life in some wonderful place abroad.

'Do you know,' he said, 'I could so easily divert some of the large sums of money that go through the accounts into a separate, secret account. More people than you can imagine have no idea how much money they have. If one decided to plan carefully it would be possible to collect enough money, deposit it in somewhere like a Swiss bank, to obtain a false passport, find some place abroad and spend the rest of one's life in comfort.'

Tom then told the story of the rich man who had forgotten that he had already handed over a large sum for an investment and had handed over another.

'There are also people who have suddenly acquired money through a will and have no idea what to do with it. They see our advertisements and ask for an interview. All one has to do is to advise them what to do with it.'

Nancy had very little idea what Tom was talking about and thought perhaps the drinks had gone to his head, but she was happy to listen. After all, she had nothing else to do and the idea of a lazy life on a South Sea island sounded the next thing to heaven.

'Did you manage to talk to your wife on the phone after all?' Nancy asked suddenly.

'Yes. She was so relieved to hear from me, she had been worried, she didn't argue and just said, "Yes dear, I am sure that is the best idea".' The two enjoyed a laugh together. Tom was already half-asleep and was pleased to stretch himself on the large settee and was soon asleep.

Nancy, who seemed not unused to this kind of situation, gathered up a series of cushions and curled up on the floor.

Elaine felt very worried. It was the first time that Tom had stayed away overnight. She had recognized the secretary's voice in the afternoon. She had heard it before but somehow this time it had seemed to contain a different note. Instead of the usual clipped professional tone announcing that Mr Westlake might be a little late tonight, there seemed to be a kind of gloating, teasing note in the voice. Polite as usual it said, 'Mrs Westlake, your husband asked me to say he will be late tonight,' and then she was almost sure that she heard a giggle.

I do hope this is nothing to do with the 'get rich quick' plan he was talking about. Somehow I don't like the sound of that girl's voice, and wild visions of Tom taking a hotel room for the night started to occupy Elaine's mind. She found it difficult to sleep and rose early, took a shower and prepared breakfast. After several cups of tea she felt better but could not manage to eat the breakfast she had prepared. She tried to busy herself tidying up the already tidy house but when ten o'clock came she could wait no longer and telephoned Tom's office.

Nancy answered the phone and said, 'Mr Westlake is in his office, I will put you through.'

The voice sounded its usual businesslike self and soon she heard Tom's voice.

'Tom. Oh, thank goodness you are all right. I have been so worried.'

'What about, surely I don't have to report every move to you? I shall be home around the usual time I expect. I have several calls to make and can't say exactly. Yes, I am quite well and please stop bothering me, I am very busy.'

Tom put down the phone not too gently. A little later he was on his way to see a wealthy client. As he drove along his brain continued to work along the lines that the evening spent in the company of Nancy had started. He felt sure that she would be only too happy to join up with him on his great adventure. He began to calculate how much money would make it worth his while to decamp with Nancy and take up residence elsewhere. Several hundred pounds, anyway, he decided, or rather several hundred thousand. A million would be better. Then sanity said, What shall I do about Elaine? I must give her another chance before I decide to go ahead with my plans. I cannot just leave and go right away without her, in any case she knows what I am thinking and could give me away if she felt very hurt and upset about it. I know she loves me, but does she love me enough to come with me?

15

Jack and Janet had settled together in the cottage. It took several days to take up the old routine but each felt so happy to be in each other's company that life, after such an ordeal, seemed almost too good to be true.

'Shall we stay here at the cottage do you think?' asked Janet.

'Oh yes, I could never think of leaving here, Mother loved the place, she had spent all her married life here, you know.'

'Yes darling, I agree with you, but we must clear out lots of old things. There are clothes lying about all over the place, your mother was not over-tidy, poor dear. Don't worry, I will be able to do if it you can manage at the garage for a day or two without me.'

'Of course, besides I want you to take it easy for a bit, you have had a hard and very worrying time. It may help you, rearranging the house, it will take your mind off all you have been through. Don't try to move any heavy thing or to move anything that needs lifting. There will be the old desk that Mother kept her letters in to be sorted out. I will try to do that tonight. The deeds of the cottage will be in there. I have got to find the key first, what a one Mother was for losing and forgetting things.'

'Yes, I am not looking forward to clearing out her bedroom. Just think what could have happened if that letter she left in that book had been lost for good.'

'That doesn't bear thinking about,' Jack said. 'And remember, I don't want to hear you talking about anything like that again. We must forget it ever happened.'

The two were so happy together they could scarcely believe their luck.

Several days passed and Janet, happily planning new curtains and covers, splendid with roses to make her lovely cottage still lovelier, but getting a bit bored at being alone in the house, put on an old overall and turned up at the garage to help. She took pleasure in all the work that she had previously thought dirty and uninteresting. It was so lovely to be free, to feel well, and to have a loving husband. To have no hidden secrets for the first time in many years. It seemed too good to be true somehow.

They went home together that evening and Jack said that he would again search for the key to Mother's desk. Janet helped in the search and under a pile of old clothes they came across Mother's old handbag. In it was a bunch of keys and together they went to the huge old desk and tried one in the lock. Soon they found the key and lifted the top. In the various pigeon-holes they found various paid bills and old letters, some stamps and lots of little things, but nothing of note. Then they unlocked the first drawer and a large folder came to light. It contained the deeds of the cottage. Searching further, a very large envelope appeared addressed to Jack. With trembling hands the excited fellow took out several large packets and a letter addressed to himself. Together they read the letter. It informed them that there was a will and named a solicitor. Another long envelope appeared, the contents of which neither could understand.

There were some certificates of some kind and a great deal of money seemed to be involved. They decided to make an appointment to see a solicitor as soon as possible to find out what all the papers were about.

That night they could scarcely sleep and next morning they were early at the garage and on the tick of ten am Jack telephoned the solicitor to make an appointment. The solicitor said that he had been expecting to hear from them but everything had been automatically left to Jack and there had really been no great hurry. He said that he had telephoned the house several times but there had been no reply. Jack replied that they were not often at home during the day.

After lunch they set out together and reached the solicitor's office in good time and asked for Mr Harrison. They were shown into his office at once. He was a rather jolly looking elderly gentleman and he greeted them both with a warm handshake.

'I was sorry to hear that your mother had died,' he said. 'I had known her a long time. She was a stubborn old lady really, and I expect you will want to call in the mortgage now.'

He looked at the two mystified people and said, 'I don't blame you, I don't think that would be the best thing to do under the circumstances.'

Jack just sat and stared at him.

'The ready cash will do you far more good than the small rate of interest your mother was satisfied with. Of course, she had been a lifetime friend of old Mrs Hands and would no take any more. However, the house is worth a great deal of money now and I am sure that I can persuade old Mrs Hands to leave it and to go to live with one of her daughters or perhaps to go into a home, she must be well over ninety now.'

At last the old fellow came to a stop, seeing the astonishment in the eyes of the young couple who obviously knew nothing of what he had been talking about.

Jack said at once, 'I have no idea at all what you are talking about. Does our cottage not belong to us?'

'Oh dear,' said Mr Harrison, and taking the bundle of papers he shuffled them apart and drew one piece of foolscap out of its envelope. 'These are the deeds of a house lived in by an old lady friend of your late mother. I believe that she was related to your father in some way. A very long time ago your mother lent her the money to buy the house, in fact she bought the house and I fixed up the loan. Mrs Hands had been paying this meagre rent. The house must now be worth £70,000 at least, perhaps more. Would you like me to see Mrs Hands or her son, who is quite well-off now actually, and to tell them that you would like to call in the money, in fact to sell the house?'

Jack scarcely knew what to say, then, after a look at Janet he gave an encouraging nod. 'Yes, I would like to sell the house but I could not turn that old lady out if my mother wished her to live there. Perhaps we could raise the rent?'

'I will see what I can do,' replied Mr Harrison. 'There is little to do about the will, as all is yours.'

The two left the solicitor's office as in a dream. They returned to the garage still wondering and both were very relieved when the time came to close up and go home.

Janet soon made some tea and then the inevitable question arose.

'What shall we do with the money?' Jack could scarcely hide his excitement. 'We will have to invest it, I suppose, or perhaps we could buy a garage of our own now.'

'There would scarcely be enough to buy a garage,' put in Janet, and they both laughed. 'Perhaps we could invest it and go on working, then look out for a place to buy. I rather fancy a village shop, at least it would be cleaner, I get fed up at times with all the black grease that seems to get on to everything,' said Janet.

Jack looked rather alarmed. 'I have always been interested in motorcars, I would not fancy anything else to earn my living at.'

'All right. By the way, we mustn't keep the money in the house when we get it.'

'Of course not. We shall put it in the bank, you know that.'

They were much too excited to go to bed and sat up very late. The result was that a hurried breakfast had to be taken next morning and they arrived at the garage just in time to see the owner drive up. He usually made a surprise visit, not planned they felt sure, but his movements were always very uncertain. After a quick look through the books he said that he was quite pleased with the way the couple worked and was thinking about giving them a small rise. Janet was very excited at the thought that they might be able to have a garage business of their own. The owner could see that she was very excited and asked if all was well.

'Yes, very well,' replied Janet. 'Actually we have had a lovely surprise.' She could no longer keep the good news to herself. 'We have inherited some money. My husband's mother died suddenly and we find that she owned another house as well as our cottage. Our solicitor has arranged to sell it and we shall have the money. We might try to buy some kind of business for ourselves.'

'I am very pleased to hear this news, of course, my dear but I hope it does not mean that you will be leaving me.'

'We haven't decided what to do with it yet. Jack told me not to tell anyone so please don't tell him that you know about it.' Already she realized that she had spoken too soon.

'Of course my dear, I promise that I will not tell him, but if you will take my advice you will invest the money. A business is a very risky thing these days, as you know there is really very little money made at this place when all the outgoings are settled. I own other places too and by the time all overheads and outgoings are settled there is not a lot left.'

When he had left Janet went to see what Jack was doing and found him working underneath a car. He asked the time and said that he would be pleased when it was closing time. All the excitement of the good news had kept them awake for so long during the night and he felt sleepy now. Janet agreed and told him about the promise of a rise in wages. She also was glad that it was nearing closing time.

'I am not so excited at the prospect of a rise as I would have been a few days ago, money seems less valuable when you have lots of it,' said Jack laughing.

'Come now,' replied Janet. 'You are not exactly a rich man now. I was wondering what we could do with the money and I was looking through some papers recently, you remember, those that came in by post, they were about investing money. They were of no interest to us then as we had no money to invest, but we have now.'

'You had better see if you can find the papers then, we may find out what to do with the money.'

'I have got one of them here, and it says that people who invested money with them seven years ago have more than doubled the amount by now.'

'They must be very clever then, my building society money has not shown that kind of profit even over more years than that. Of course it is a very small amount anyway. We will have plenty of time to talk about the money when we get it.'

Janet returned to the office and prepared to close up for the day.

16

Tom Westlake was astounded at the careless way his client spoke about investments.

'I can't go wrong if I invest this lot with you then,' he said to Tom. 'You have always produced quite wonderful results and I never even look at the literature you send me now. I am sure I can't do better than leave it in your hands,' and he promptly handed over a very large cheque.

'What do you want to invest in this time?' asked Tom.

'I don't really want to be bothered with a lot of figures I don't understand,' he replied. 'I am quite happy to leave it to you. I have, as you will seem, made the cheque out to you and I am sure you will see that the money is invested to best advantage.' He then looked at his watch and started to get up from his chair. 'I am a very busy man. I would ask you to stay to lunch but I am wanted elsewhere, I am afraid.'

'That's quite all right, I have several calls to make myself,' replied Tom.

Tom made several less fruitful calls then started for home. Stopping the car he took out the cheque he had been handed and looked at it. £1,00,000 pounds. I can scarcely believe it. Now could be my chance. I can delay a short time before cashing this cheque. I wonder how long would be safe? I can always say I forgot to pass it in if anyone asks about it. I must see if there is any further hope of obtaining another large amount before I hand it in, tomorrow I have two possibilities but I must see Elaine and have a talk with her. It will be her own fault if she will not go along with me. I don't really trust Nancy, but I can't carry the whole plan through without someone to help me.

Tom made two more calls and spent some very unfruitful time

as he realized that if his plans were successful he would not have enough time to turn any further money his way. He decided to go home early to Elaine, hoping finally to persuade her to join him in the project. After all, he reminded himself, she must realize it means losing a husband if she decides against going along with me.

Elaine was not expecting Tom so early. She had felt very hurt and unhappy when he didn't come home last evening. She did not like his tone on the telephone but kept telling herself that it was probably her imagination. Tom often had to eat out with a client and really it was very thoughtful of him to refrain from driving after he had taken alcohol. It was much safer to spend the night elsewhere. There were many small hotels in town or perhaps a client had asked him to stay overnight. It had happened before but she had to admit to herself that he had never before asked someone else to make his excuses.

Tom drove straight into the garage and walked into the house. Elaine heard him and rushed to meet him.

'Oh, darling, I am so glad you are all right, I have been so worried. Don't think I blame you for staying in town, you were very wise.' She clung to him and kissed him again and again.

'There's no need to make such a fuss, I'm here now and I'm very hungry, what is there to eat?'

'I can soon have a meal ready, it is so good to have you at home. I have been so worried.'

She hurried off to the kitchen to rush together the best meal she could produce at such short notice.

The meal was soon over and then Tom said that they must have a serious talk. 'I shall be going away out of the country quite soon and I would like to take you with me.'

Elaine tried to speak but Tom waved her away.

'Wait until you hear the full story. I have acquired, or rather I have been presented with a large sum of money and it will lie idle for a long time if invested. Perhaps it will never be used. It will be easy for me to borrow this money and to leave the country with it.' Tom deliberately used the word 'borrow' as he thought it sounded better than 'acquire'.

Elaine looked at him in surprise, she knew that he was talking about money belonging to clients, handed over for investments, but realized that if she started to disagree with him he would still go ahead and would go without her if necessary. She told herself that she must use all her powers of persuasion to talk him out of the whole idea. It would be difficult, she knew, life had so far been very unrewarding for Tom. He had such charm when he liked to use it and she could not really blame him for allowing people to trust him, but it would be fatal just to let him go ahead and leave the country with money that was not his. After all, it was stealing and if he was caught it would almost certainly mean a long term of imprisonment. She could not bear to think of the results.

Tom continued to talk of his plans and named a day about ten days ahead as the day he hoped to finalize his plans and to travel. He said that he already had two very large sums of money in his possession and hoped to get at least one more. He would arrange to sell the car and have it collected from the airport. Regarding their possessions, these would have to be left in the flat as they must travel light. This way it would be kept a secret that they had left the country as long as possible.

Elaine listened to all these plans. She could not think clearly. How could Tom expect her to leave everything and fly with him to some unknown destination?

'What about our passports?' she asked.

'I will take care of those, please get yours and I will get it changed to another name right away. No one will be able to trace us and we shall be able to take up a life of luxury and comfort where living is easy and cheap.'

Elaine could see that Tom really meant to carry out his plan, what could she do? Could she ask Father? No. She felt sure that all Father would say would be: 'I never liked him anyway, you must leave him.'

Fearful of upsetting Tom, Elaine kept silent for a long time and listened to more plans then said, 'I must have a few days to think about it dear, I promise that I will give it careful thought. All I want is for us to be happy together. I am used now to being short of money and things will change soon.' Then, seeing Tom's face begin to cloud over again, she went to fetch her passport.

Tom arrived at the office next day to find Nancy very welcoming with a warm and friendly smile and his letters in her hand. It was her job to sort the post and many clients preferred to deal with Tom. They would write to him in preference to the company by name. Another client had asked for advice about investing a large sum of money. Nancy had read the letters, he had no doubt, and he tried to remember how much he had confided in her. Had he told her all his plans? He knew that yesterday he had felt very angry with Elaine for trying to dissuade him from his wonderful project.

Nancy seemed to imply that she knew all as she tapped the most promising letter with her highly polished nails and said, 'Shall I make an appointment for you tomorrow, if possible?'

Tom read the letter and could see that it was very tempting. 'Yes, I think so if you can,' he replied.

A little later when they had the office to themselves Nancy came up to him and said, 'I am with you all the way if you do decide to carry out the plan you spoke about, you can count on me.'

Tom was somewhat taken aback at this disclosure. Whilst he did not feel too sure that Elaine would go along with him, she was his wife and he had to consider her first. 'All right, Nancy,' he replied rather coldly, 'I will bear in mind what you say. I am rather busy just now,' and he buried himself in a mountain of papers.

Next day was Sunday and almost all day Tom talked to Elaine about his plans. To Elaine it was the most miserable day she had ever spent. She was too worried to give a definite answer and so she let it appear that she was prepared to go. She handed over her passport when pressed to.

'I have a very large cheque to change and we might have to leave in a hurry,' Tom said.

* * *

On Monday the first letter that Jack opened was from Mr Harrison.

'Look at this,' he shouted to Janet who was in the kitchen getting breakfast. 'The old lady's son is happy to pay £60,000 for the house. It seems that he was unaware that the house was not his mother's. He is a builder and he brought the cheque in his hand. Mr Harrison also says that we should ask more for the house, what do you think?'

'I should think that the money paid right away is the best and we should not argue.'

'I agree with you,' said Jack. 'After all, you agree that my mother wished the old lady happiness and being greedy about the money for the house is not what she would have wished. Shall I go over and pay it into the bank?'

'I think that is a good idea, then we can think what we can do with it. I have been thinking about that folder that came through the post recently about advice over investments we could get free. Actually, I saw an advertisement the next day by the same people, they said that money could be doubled in a very short time, about six years they said. Shall I make an appointment if I can find the folder?'

'All right,' said Jack. 'There is no harm in finding out what they have to say.'

Jack was still floating on air and could have said 'yes' to almost anything. 'Fix it up for tomorrow afternoon if you can, and I will be here then.'

Janet found the brochure and went to the telephone. A pleasant voice answered which actually belonged to Nancy. She said that she knew which folder was being referred to and felt sure that much information and help with investments was available and she would try to make an appointment for an adviser to call tomorrow. 'I will ring back,' she said, and a little later she did so and an appointment was made for an adviser to call the next afternoon.

Janet was jubilant and ran out into the garage to tell Jack who was looking at the worksheet fastened to a large car.

'Lots to do here,' he said as Janet approached.

'I have good news dear, I have fixed up for a man to call tomorrow afternoon about three o'clock.'

'What about?' asked Jack.

'You know, silly, the money.'

'All right, remind me again in the morning,' teased Jack as he crawled under a large car.

* * *

Tom was well aware that he had a hard task ahead to persuade Elaine to agree to his plan of action. He tried hard to keep out of Nancy's way at the office. Fortunately he was out most of the time, and when Nancy told him that she had fixed up an interesting appointment for him in the country on Tuesday morning with a knowing look, he was reminded again that he had been rather silly to confide his aims and plans to her, but after all he might yet need her. He was still not quite sure how much he had told Nancy. This reminded him that he must get the two passports changed. He had heard of a man who was prepared to do all kinds of things for money. He had laughed at the time, he remembered, but all the same he had made a note of the address. This man was supposed to be able to produce a ten pound note that would defy detection in a poor light. Tom did not want ten pound notes but something that was just as important to him at present. He realized as he went looking for the address that he had made his decision and could not now look back.

I suppose I could say that I had lost our passports if this project does not go through, he consoled himself. There was only one thing to do, time was short, people might start to miss the large amounts that they had handed over to him in cheque form if he delayed too long before paying them in.

Tom reassured himself that what he wanted was nothing really. Each time he had travelled abroad by air his passport had been scarcely looked at. One glance at the photograph and then at him and the passport had been handed straight back. He was soon on his way to see the obliging forger, if forging it could be called. After several times looking up and down the dingy street he finally decided that the address he had been given was this dirty overcrowded little shop, full of what looked like old rubbish with various price tags attached. Tom entered and asked if he could talk to someone about passports.

'I am perhaps the man you want,' said a dirty looking man who peered over a screen.

'I am not sure if I have come to the right place really. A friend said that you might help me with some passports.'

'What makes your friend say that, I wonder? Who are you anyway? You might be a Scotland Yard officer for all I know.'

'No, my dear chap, I can soon convince you as to my credentials. I merely need the names changed on my passports. You see, my wife and I have agreed to take over a holiday booking that my friend and his wife made to go to Australia. They can't go. The tickets are in their names and we can't do anything about it. We would hate to miss the chance of such a holiday.'

The man cast his eyes up and down over Tom's clothes, his shoes, and finally his face. 'It sounds like a good story,' he said, 'show me proof of your identity.

'Well,' said Tom, 'here are the passports for a start and here is my driving licence and my Trustcard. You will see that I am genuine. Furthermore, how do I know that I can trust you?'

The man smiled in an oily kind of way and took the cards. He looked at the passports. 'What about the photographs?' he asked.

'They will be all right, I told you, I only want the names changed.'

'It will cost you £25 each,' said the man, 'in advance.'

'I will pay you when I collect them,' said Tom.

'All right, what name do you want? Smith, I suppose.'

'No, I had not really thought about that.'

Suddenly he thought of Nancy, there was an uncanny resemblance to his wife Elaine. Should it turn out after all that Elaine would not go with him, Nancy could easily pass as the traveller whose face was pictured on the passport. Especially if the hairstyle was slightly changed. Then again, his first thought regarding a name was dangerous. He had thought of using Nancy's name but could easily be traced if things went wrong. In his heart he longed for Elaine to agree to his plan. He realized that he really loved her and thought with dismay that life would never be really happy without her. He knew that Nancy would soon get on his nerves. She was not his idea of a perfect partner but, he consoled himself, there were plenty of nice girls about who would be only too pleased to make themselves pleasant to a man who had money. The man was waiting for his answer.

'What do you suggest?'

'Let's have a look at the name, it could be Westland, or Willard, without much trouble.'

'All right,' replied Tom. 'Mr and Mrs Westland it shall be. When can I have them?'

'Wednesday afternoon all right?'

'Yes, I will call then.' Tom hastily left the shop and was soon on his way back to the office.

That evening he again began to enlarge on the subject of leaving everything to travel abroad. 'Are you going to come with me Elaine? I want you to but I can't order you to. Tell me please, will you come or not? I warn you, you may never see me again if you don't. When I am gone you might have a lot of unpleasantness fired at you, what will you do if you are left here alone?'

'You really mean to go then?' asked Elaine.

She could now see that Tom was really in earnest and also that she had to make a definite decision at once. Never had a woman been faced with such a dilemma, she thought, it was either be hanged or shot. No, not so bad as that, after all life might not be so bad in the lovely warm climate Tom had pictured. Did Tom really love her? Was all this planning he was doing really possible, was it workable? It sounded sheer madness to her, but he was supposed to be the one with the brains. Did Tom really love her? Surely he could not talk so glibly about going without her if he didn't. If he didn't it would be much better for her to stay here where she had at least a few friends than find herself amongst a lot of holiday loving strangers. Tom would love it there, she knew. He was such an easygoing fellow, welcome in any circle. Everybody liked him. Except Father. What would Father say if they suddenly disappeared? Then sanity returned. I must make my decision, she told herself, what can I say?

'You must say yes or no tomorrow,' Tom had said before he left home that morning. 'I intend to book two passages to travel either on Saturday or next Monday, whichever I can get a short notice,' and he waved her a casual goodbye.

17

On Tuesday morning Janet reminded Jack that the man was coming to talk about investments at three o'clock and Jack said, 'Oh, I thought of going for a drive. You are the one with the brains, surely you can talk to him.'

Janet began to look worried and Jack hurried to reassure her. 'Of course I shall be here,' he said, 'with my boots blacked. I am a man of some means now, you know, you are the wife of an important man. All right, I shall be here at three o'clock.'

At three o'clock Janet was feeling rather nervous. 'Will the man come — ' then, looking out of the window she saw a car draw up on the opposite side of the road. The number plate seemed to stand out to her as she read it. There were her own initials at the end. Perhaps that will be an omen, she thought. As she watched a tall, good-looking man got out of the car and looked around. Quickly she left the window and went to open the door. 'Do come in Mr . . . .'

'Westlake,' Tom added. 'What a lovely cottage.'

He was at his best, a really charming fellow, Janet thought. Tom shook hands and followed her into the cosy little sitting room, soon he was shaking hands with Jack and complimenting him on owning such a delightful cottage. 'It is yours I suppose?' he said, looking round.

'Oh yes,' said Jack, 'my mother died recently and left it to me.'

'I see, is that what you wish to do? Sell the cottage and invest the money?'

He stood up, walked across the room and looked out of the rear window which gave a view over the garden with a calculating look on his face. 'It should fetch a good price,' he continued.

Jack and Janet looked at each other, trying to gather their astonished thoughts. 'Oh no,' they both said at once. 'We live here,' said Janet, 'but we have been left a large sum, or rather a large house which is worth a lot of money, and we thought of selling it and investing the money, we saw a leaflet which you sent to us by post and it said that we could make three times the money if we invested it and we thought it was better than starting a business, didn't we Jack?'

Jack came to life at last, he was always rather slow in the uptake, as Janet told him sometimes, and it was a good thing that she was able to respond quickly at times whilst he thought things out. Janet was astonished at herself now for blurting out all their thoughts and looked at Jack appealingly.

'Yes,' went on Jack. 'You see, we work at the garage and whilst my wife can easily cope with the booking and I am a good mechanic we do not really have the confidence to risk all the money on a business for ourselves.'

'Oh, I see, I quite understand,' said Tom with an easy and almost fatherly manner. 'Let me advise you, actually that is what I am here for isn't it? How much do you think the house is worth if you manage to sell it?'

'Oh, we can sell it all right,' said Jack. 'The occupier has already offered £60,000 for it, cash, and we have agreed to accept. We shall most probably have the cash tomorrow. We could have got more if we had vacant possession to offer, but an old lady lives there with her son, she was a friend of my late mother and I could not turn her out.'

'That is why you want to know the best way to invest the money, I suppose,' replied Tom.

'Yes, we can't just leave it lying in the bank, we thought of a building society but . . . where is that folder darling,' and Jack started to look around for the brochure which Tom was quite conversant with.

'You mean to let my firm invest it for you?' he put in. 'Yes, we may be able to get almost twice the amount for you that any building society would offer, of course we make no promises but if you let us have the money to manage for you we will invest it in whatever is available at the time to the best advantage for you. You can either arrange to draw a regular income from it or leave it to accumulate until such time as you want to make some other use of it.'

Tom proceeded to talk at length very glowingly about all kinds of things that neither Jack nor Janet had ever heard of, and each felt rather conscious of their ignorance. At length, after a cup of tea, Tom said that he must go.

'I don't know what my boss will say to me for spending so much time talking to one customer, my time is quite valuable he thinks,' he said with a laugh. 'Here's my card, that's my address, you can send your cheque to me for my personal attention, or of course to the firm direct. In that case it may take a little longer for someone to handle the account. We are a very highly regarded firm of stockbrokers, you know, and if you decide to let us handle your account you can't go wrong. If I am in charge of it I promise that I will give it my personal attention and get it placed to your best advantage at once. It is a good time now and the sooner the better. Would you like me to call round again perhaps? I shall be free tomorrow afternoon if you think you will have the money through by then.'

Tom left the house having great difficulty in hiding his laughter. Were there really such simple trusting people left in the present day world? What was their lawyer doing? Or were they too careful to employ one? He sat down in his car and congratulated himself. 'Here is another £60,000 just waiting for me to pick up.'

'What do you think, Jack?'

'Oh, he seems all right, a decent sort of chap. I think we shall be doing right to let him invest the money for us. We are lucky really that you did not throw that folder away, let's have a look at his card, it must be nice having a printed card of your own. Perhaps I shall have one some day.'

'More likely a greasy worksheet,' replied Janet laughing.

She knew that Jack loved his work and was never happier than when he was underneath a car, unless it was when he was driving one.

They soon got back to work again, each thinking about how easy it was to invest money in a profitable way. You just had to know the right people.

When the telephone rang Janet did not rush to answer it at once. At the moment there was plenty of work waiting at the garage and sometimes it became difficult to placate people who so often wanted some job done to their car at once. One had to be almost an expert at public relations at times. The phone went on ringing and rather reluctantly Janet picked it up. It was Mr Harrison with good news. He said that he had accepted a cash payment for their house and had the cheque.

Janet could scarcely hide her excitement. 'What is the figure?' she asked.

'The one we agreed upon, £60,000,' replied Mr Harrison. 'You could perhaps have got more on the open market but you may not have been able to get them out.'

'I quite understand,' said Janet. 'I am sure Jack will come in and get it very soon.'

She almost ran into the workshop with the good news and Jack said that he had a car ready for a trial run so he would go right away and collect the cheque.

That evening, after a very late meal, Jack said that it was a pity they did not have the money when Tom Westlake was with them. He felt quite confident that they could not do better than let him handle the money. After all, they knew nothing about finance, except perhaps garage workshop and hire-car business. Janet reminded him that Tom Westlake had said he would call again for the money when they had it if they liked.

'Why not telephone him tonight?' Janet seemed keen and said, 'You have his home address, you could ask him if he would like to call for the money, perhaps tomorrow. After all, you could write him a cheque. Long before he goes to cash it, you will have paid this one into the bank.'

This sounded like a good idea to Jack and he went at once to try to telephone Tom Westlake.

* * *

Tom Westlake decided that he had done enough business for the day and went home rather early. Elaine was surprised to see him so early and hoped that he would not bring up the subject of leaving again. She still could not believe that he really meant to go but after a tasty and well-cooked meal was disposed of in silence, Tom asked her to come and sit down to talk. 'I really must know your answer,' he said. 'I have to collect our passports tomorrow and I have had a wonderful piece of good luck today. Another large sum of money is mine for the taking within a day or two and the prospect tomorrow of several more sums of investment. Now will you agree to come? You will have a lovely time, I promise you. You have nothing to lose. I would rather take you than anyone else.'

Elaine looked sharply up at this remark. 'What do you mean? Anyone else? You speak as if you had someone else lined up and ready to go.'

Tom was stung by this remark, it was too near the truth. At that moment the telephone rang and Elaine went to answer.

'It is for you,' she said.

Tom was delighted to say that he would be only too happy to call on the Willards at their garage tomorrow to pick up their cheque. He would bring a receipt and would let them know in a very short time what shares he had chosen for them. He returned to Elaine with the remark, 'There, that is another large cheque waiting for me to collect tomorrow.'

He felt a stab of shame as she looked at him, obviously still hurt at his remark about taking someone else. Then he thought, it's her own fault if she won't come with me, I have risked all for her, and for myself too. He tried to hide from himself any feelings of guilt and shame he felt towards his wife but he could not understand how his partner in life, who had always been so amenable until this crisis, had suddenly changed. She had very much wanted to have a child. Tom had put his foot down at once at this idea. Otherwise she had agreed to everything he had suggested. Their marriage had been happy, it had always been nice to come home, no matter how late, to a loving welcoming wife and tasty well-cooked meal. Elaine had never questioned his handling of the money, she always seemed to manage on the small allowance he made for housekeeping and he knew that sometimes she would walk miles in order to purchase fruit or vegetables that seemed fresher or perhaps more economical. Often in the evening she would be busy sewing some shapeless thing, and if ever he was interested enough to enquire she would say perhaps that it was a sheet that she was turning sides-to-middle or one of his shirts that she was giving a new ready-made collar that she had painstakingly matched up. He knew that life would have been much harder with a less competent and helpful wife. Never mind, he told himself, if I do have to take Nancy I shall not be poor enough to have to ask her to economize. In any case I would have no liability towards her. The last thing I would ever do is to ask her to marry me.

It seemed no use talking to Elaine any longer and Tom suggested going to bed. Elaine agreed and said, 'You go up. I have some clearing up to do.'

Tom very thankfully went to bed but found that he was quite unable to go to sleep. After tossing and turning for a long time he realized that it was after midnight and Elaine had not yet come to bed. She must have fallen asleep by the fire, he told himself, and tried again to sleep. Suddenly he thought of the hot malted milk that Elaine usually mixed for their bedtime drink. He got up and went to the kitchen. Finding the jar almost empty he scraped out enough, he thought, to make himself a drink and boiled the kettle. He took his drink to the sitting room and there, to his astonishment, lay Elaine on the large old-fashioned sofa with a rug over her and a cushion for her head.

He took a step towards her thinking to wake her up. His steps were inaudible on the carpet and she slept on. Turning slowly away he retired again alone. If Elaine chose to sleep alone she could have the bed, and indeed the whole flat to herself after tonight.

When morning dawned he tried to gather all his confused thoughts. Suddenly he realized that Elaine knew all his plans. It could be quite dangerous to leave her behind if he left the country for good, especially if he took Nancy with him. Elaine knew more or less all his plans and although he did not think she would ever be spiteful towards him he could not be sure that she would not, in her anger and jealousy, say something, even if inadvertently to enable him to be traced. Whilst packing up his clothes and a few items of value a sudden idea occurred to him. He would call at the house this afternoon and carry out a plan that seemed almost cast-iron to him. If he planned it carefully nothing could very well go wrong. Elaine usually went out during the afternoon and he could arrange to call at the house unobserved whilst she was out.

Having made his plans, which he now thought was brilliant, he set off towards the Willard's garage to collect his first contribution for the day.

Jack and Janet greeted him excitedly and he followed them into the office. 'Here is a receipt for your cheque,' he said. 'Particulars of what your money will be invested in will follow in a few days.'

Jack took the form. It looked important. He sat down at the desk and wrote out the cheque and handed it over importantly.

'Thank you,' said Tom, 'may this be the start of a very happy and prosperous relationship for us.'

He turned away then and said, 'Do you mind if I leave right away? I have a great many calls to make today.'

'Of course not,' replied Jack, 'I am a busy man too.'

They shook hands and Tom hurried away.

Tom did not have much luck with his other professional calls and decided to concentrate on carrying out his plan. The one he had suddenly thought of in desperation upon realizing that Elaine might be a danger to him. Elaine was often out during the day and would almost certainly be seen by some friend or other today. Friends would see her alive and well. A desperate idea had occurred suddenly to his active brain. Elaine always made a mug of hot milk for herself every night at bedtime. His idea was a brainwave, why not purchase some kind of poison that would mix undetected with the milk powder in the jar? He had noticed last night that there was very little milk powder in the jar. No doubt Elaine would rinse out the jar for her last evening drink tonight.

The next call Tom made was to a small private chemist. He had never been there before and was not known. A girl came forward and Tom said, 'Could I see someone about how to get rid of a very old dog painlessly that is sick and ill?'

The girl looked surprised and went to fetch a young man who looked quite professional in his white coat. Tom made the same request and the young man looked very surprised. 'I would have thought a vet would be the best one to deal with that,' he said.

'Yes, I know, but the vet is not able to do something for some time, he is so busy. The dog is old, ill and in pain and we are afraid that he might bite someone. If I could have some kind of powder that is easy to dissolve in milk and be undetected. He will take milk and is always thirsty.'

Looking at the chemist, Tom could see that he was reluctant to prescribe anything in such a flimsy way. Tom continued, 'He is pretty intelligent and it would not be possible for him to take a pill.'

'I will see what I can do,' said the man reluctantly. He started to look along his shelves. 'There's arsenic, of course, we can only sell it if prescribed or in a weed-killer, would that do?'

'No, I'm afraid not,' replied Tom.

Suddenly the man said, 'Here is a white powder that contains arsenic,' reaching down a small white jar. 'It is rather expensive but you would not require very much. A pinch would do, I would think. How big is the dog? I would think that a pinch dissolved in warm milk in a small bowl would have the desired effect and if the dog is dangerous perhaps it would be the best way of dealing with it. Have you got it tied up?'

'Oh yes, we had to shut him up when he got dangerous in case he bit someone.'

'You will have to sign the poison book, I am afraid. Regulations.'

'Of course,' said Tom and got out his pen. It would be quite easy to give a false name and address. He was not known around here at all. He left the shop with the packet stowed away in his pocket.

Arriving back home with his purchase Tom found that Elaine was not at home, she had possibly gone shopping or was calling on a neighbour, although he knew that she did not make friends very easily in this district.

He was able to go into the kitchenette, take the almost empty jar from the shelf and shake the small pinch of powder into it, mixing it carefully with the spoonful of powder left in the jar.

Tom felt no compunction about destroying his wife, somehow his mind was set on one course only and he was not able to accept the fact that anyone or anything could get in his way.

He had two very large cheques which he intended to cash at the bank forthwith and his salary was due. He had already diverted many varied amounts into his own account and altogether he should have enough cash to last him in a land that was poor but beautiful for a long time.

He searched around for the last of his possessions that were easy to carry, placed them in his car and left the house for good without leaving a note. As he travelled on his way back to the office he did his best to train his mind away from thinking of his wife. The happy times they had had together over the years and the plans they had made which were so long in showing any sign of coming to fruition. That part of his life was over and done with. He managed almost to convince himself that Elaine would be better dead than alive to face a long struggle alone, faced with recriminations as she reminded herself of what she had missed by being so stubborn and unhelpful to her husband.

On his arrival at the office Nancy greeted him with effusion. He dispatched her to her own office with a long list of letters which needed her attention then he proceeded to contact Heathrow Airport. He enquired about tickets to travel on Saturday or before, what had they got to offer? One way only, abroad. He was told that it was too late to book for any country except perhaps a short route, the best thing he could so was to come to the airport and hope to get a standby ticket. Sometimes people are unable to travel and have to cancel at almost the last minute.

'Where exactly did you want to go?' she asked.

Tom was a little vague and wished that he had studied the map of the world a little more closely. Geography was not his strong subject by any means, and he found it difficult to recall the vague plans he had made without a map, he needed some time to work out what might be a favourable country.

'Just a minute,' said the clerk. 'I have two cancellations for Hong Kong. They are first-class and will be costly but I can reserve them for you if it is urgent that you leave the country.'

'I wish you would, please,' replied Tom.

'Can I have your name and address then please? You will leave at ten am on Saturday. Will you call and collect the tickets as soon as you can please, or I may not be able to holed them.'

'All right, I will arrange to collect them as soon as I can. My name is — ' and Tom was just about to give his name when he remembered that he had not collected the passports and furthermore the names he had agreed upon had temporarily gone out of his mind.

'Just a moment,' he said, 'I will ring you back,' and put the phone down. He saw that Nancy was standing in front of his desk and was staring at him. He didn't think that she could have heard what he had been saying, he pulled forward a pad of paper and began to write. I know it began with W. Westland? That was it, T. Westland and E. Westland.

Waiting until Nancy had left his office he again dialled the airport and gave the two names, promising that he would collect the tickets as soon as he possibly could. I really must go and collect those passports, he told himself, and hurriedly looked through the correspondence on his desk. There seemed to be nothing that needed immediate attention and he sat back to collect his thoughts. Suddenly a thought struck him.

I must go home tonight, I can't let Elaine take that powder tonight. It is too soon. I could be found out and traced tomorrow, before I get a chance to get abroad. What shall I do? I really can't face Elaine again, I will have to disappear tomorrow. I wonder if I can take Nancy into my confidence safely? She could hide me until tomorrow and then we will be ready to go if she will agree. I wonder if I can trust her?

With this thought he sent for Nancy and said, 'I have to go out, I can't talk to you about my plans here, what about dinner tonight?'

'Well,' said Nancy. Feeling rather hurt that Tom had pushed her away before, she hesitated. Then, seeing the look on Tom's face she said hurriedly, 'You can take me out for a meal if you can come back to my place.'

'All right,' said Tom, 'I have to go out now but I will pick you up about six when you are ready to leave.'

Nancy agreed to this suggestion and Tom set off for the seedy looking shop where the passports should be waiting. He had some compunction at leaving the car outside the shop and parked it some way away. A small boy was sitting on the pavement with his back to the wall, playing with a very battered toy train. Tom approached him and the boy looked up apprehensively.

'Don't worry,' said Tom, 'I have a small job for you. How would you like to sit there and keep an eye on my car? If you see anyone looking at it I shall be in that old shop down the road and I will give you 20p for yourself.'

'Give me the money now, Mister.'

'No, I will give you the money when you have earned it,' said Tom.

He walked off and the boy got up and walked round the car, inspecting every detail carefully, then sat down to play with his train.

Tom entered the shop and pressed the dirty bell on the even dirtier counter. The same evil looking man appeared. 'Oh, it's you. I thought you had got scared and had done a bunk without the passports,' he said sneering.

Tom held back a rejoinder as the man went to get them. 'No, I have been busy and couldn't get here before, how much did you say they would be? Ten pounds each I think?'

The man gave a murderous look. 'Fifty pounds altogether, and that's cheap, I face a very heavy fine if I am found out, probably imprisonment.'

'Don't worry, you won't be found out, let's have a look at them.'

The man handed them over reluctantly, almost as if he thought that Tom would snatch them and run out of the shop.

'Yes, they will do. Will you take a cheque?'

'No, I won't and you should know better than to ask.'

Tom produced the money, handed it over, took the passports and started to walk towards the door. 'How do I know that I can rely on you to keep quiet about this?' asked Tom.

'Don't be a fool, if I am caught so will you be. Clear off, I don't want to see hair or hide of you again.'

Tom was quick to do as suggested and walked back to his car, handing the boy the promised fee, and was soon driving thankfully out of the neighbourhood.

Soon he arrived outside the office and there stood Nancy who soon climbed into the car. 'I have been shopping and have the makings of a tasty meal. Would you like to come in and share it?'

'Well, Nancy, I was going to ask you if you could put me up tonight, I have something to discuss with you.'

Nancy was thrilled with this and could scarcely hide her excitement. She placed her parcels on the rear seat and got into the car beside Tom.

Tom made no comments about Nancy's cooking, after all there was not much encouragement to tenants of one-roomed flats. Afterwards Tom started hesitatingly to ask if he could stay overnight again. 'I have something very important to discuss with you,' he said. 'First of all, will you help me to get my luggage from the car and find somewhere to put it overnight?'

Nancy looked surprised. 'Have you left your wife then?' she asked. 'I don't know if I want to get mixed up in a divorce case, Tom.'

'No, it's nothing like that, come and help me to get the cases in and I will put you in the picture.'

They carried the luggage in and managed to stow it away.

'I want to put in a day at the office tomorrow, a morning at least; I have several calls to make in the afternoon then I shall put in an appearance but I have a lot of arrangements to make. Do you remember what we discussed before? I expect I talked a lot of drivel.'

'You said all kinds of things about going to live in a warm country for good.'

'I want to clean out the car tomorrow because if my plans go well I shall be selling it on Friday. I shall assume a different personality at the same time. Will you help me, Nancy? I promise you that I won't let you down, if you decide to throw in your lot with me you can have a wonderful time.'

'I must decide what is involved before I take any rash steps,' replied Nancy.

'I can understand your reluctance, I will tell you my plans. I am trusting you completely and putting myself in your hands. Some might say that I am taking a great risk doing this but I am sick to death of using my personality to persuade money out of other people's pockets for someone else's benefit. At times I have handled what amounted to thousands of pounds with a miserable pittance for myself at the end of it. I can spend all my best years working for someone else to get rich and end up with less than I started with. If I can make money for others I can make it for myself. I was expecting my wife to go along with me but to my astonishment she has no faith in me at all and does not apparently love me enough to trust me. I fear that she will regret it but I do not wish to be here any longer. I mean to completely disappear. I am putting myself in your hands. Will you go along with me? I promise you that you will share in a comfortable life in a beautiful land if you will help me to hide my personality and to become another man.'

Nancy was getting more and more intrigued. She pictured Tom with a false beard and dyed hair. 'All right, tell me what I have to do and I will go along with you.'

'First of all you must realize that I am no longer Tom Westlake. I am Tom Westland and you are my wife, Mrs E. Westland. I have two tickets waiting to be collected at Heathrow to travel to Hong Kong early on Saturday, so you will have very little time to arrange your affairs. You will have to give up the flat and leave your job and pack your things to be at Heathrow with me early in the morning. I have tomorrow only to wind up my affairs and arrange a transfer from my bank to one in Hong Kong. Then on Friday we will have to disappear together. We will become someone else. We can stay at a hotel near the airport for the last night. At all costs I must be someone else after tomorrow.' He looked at Nancy. 'Now you have heard my plans what do you say?'

Nancy looked bright-eyed and excited. 'I'm game, but can we pull it off?'

'We have got to pull it off. After all, London is a very big place, it should be easy to disappear here.'

'Tell me again what we do tomorrow,' said Nancy.

'First you go to the office as usual, I shall telephone in to say that I have not been well and shall have a few days off. You do your usual day's work but I will leave it to you if you work out Friday and get your pay. We shall both have to completely disappear after Friday, that is leave the district and stay elsewhere for the last night.'

'What if your wife rings in to the office tomorrow and asks to speak to you?'

'She is not likely to do that.'

'What if she does?'

'Just tell her that I am away on business. Then, get all your clothes packed ready to leave, I don't think you need any kind of disguise actually, just wear a hat and a cover-all kind of coat. I have to completely change my appearance but I have things to do first. I telephoned the bank and asked them to wind up my affairs today as I was going abroad. I also told them that I would have several large cheques to pay in tomorrow so that they would have everything ready.

'On Friday I shall change my appearance completely, perhaps you can help me there, then we leave early for the airport on Saturday. We will have excess luggage to pay for so I want you to take as little as possible. Try to discard anything that is not absolutely necessary. I did wish at one time to find some place to deposit my odds and ends but I have no wish ever to return to this country. You realize that you will not need a fur coat or any warm clothing, so leave all you can behind or sell it.'

'Don't worry about me, I don't have a fur coat anyway,' replied Nancy. 'I was out of a job for a long time you know, and I shall be happy to leave some of my shabby clothes behind.'

'You always look very smart to me, and very nice too,' replied Tom gallantly.

They both set to work and cleared out all the personal belongings from the flat and packed those that Nancy wanted to keep in her two large trunks.

'It's lucky I kept these, they have been in the way though and I have threatened to get rid of them. I must have had second sight deciding to keep them.'

Tom did not feel much like joking but Nancy was bubbling over with excitement. Here was an adventure that exceeded her wildest dreams, all planned for her. She had nothing to do but go along with it. She told herself that she had not been expected even to sleep with Tom so far, but surely it would be a very easy price to pay for the kind of life that seemed to be stretching out for her, just for the taking.

'I pay my rent quarterly so no one will miss me for some time and they are welcome to what I leave behind,' Nancy said. 'I have several days' leave due to me at the office so I will take them now.'

'Why didn't I think of that?' said Tom. 'I have already arranged that I will not be missed. I said that I have arranged to go to Yorkshire to see a client and may have to stay the night. It will be Monday before anyone at the office starts to ask where I am.'

'You seem to have arranged everything beautifully, and I do admire your business acumen and planning capabilities. Suppose we retire for the night now, it is getting very late.'

'All right,' agreed Tom.

Nancy looked hard at him and Tom began to fear that he might not be able to avoid close contact with the girl. His feelings had changed somehow. At first he had looked forward to a mild kind of flirtation with a certain amount of pleasure, but the prospect of sharing a bed with Nancy made him go hot and cold, all he wanted was somewhere to lay his weary head and sleep. His brain was teeming with thoughts. He had difficulty in keeping his imagination at bay when he reminded himself that by now Elaine would have taken a fatal dose of poison. He must not let himself think of such things, that particular thing least of all. He would otherwise think of suicide himself. The very last thing he wanted was the proximity of another woman.

They made up a bed on the settee for Tom and Nancy said, 'Good night.' She was not completely without sympathy and realized that Tom must have been pretty desperate to carry out such a co-ordinated and cold-blooded plan so efficiently.

18

Jack and Janet had spent a long day at the garage, trying to cope with all the work and trying not to talk about the excitement they had experienced investing the wonderful inheritance that Jack's mother had left them. They were still talking about their plans and about the future when Jack said, 'Don't you think we should tell Mr Harrison what we have done with the money? I am sure that he would be interested to know that we had invested it so well and not started to "fritter it away" as Mother would have said.'

'Yes, I am sure he would be interested to hear what we have done. Suppose you telephone him in the morning and tell him?'

Next day Janet's attention kept on straying until at last she decided the solicitor would be at his office, then she picked up the telephone and dialled the number. The clerk put her straight through to Mr Harrison and he sounded pleased to hear her.

'How are you both? Have you decided what to do with your small fortune yet?'

'Oh, we are very well thank you. Regarding the money, Jack thought you would like to know what we have done with it. We put the cheque straight into the bank, of course, and then this brochure appeared through the post. We had heard about these things before but as we never had any money to invest we didn't bother with it. First we thought of buying a garage business but we would also have had to borrow more to really get started. Then we had a talk with the owner of the one we work at and he said that although he owns a chain of garages he was finding it hard to keep his head above water.'

By now Mr Harrison was getting a little tired of waiting for the real news and interrupted with, 'So what did you do Mrs Willard?'

'Do you want to make an appointment to see me about it?'

'Oh, I am sorry, I am wasting your time. Well, we have invested it in stocks and shares. We answered the brochure and a very nice gentleman called and told us about how we could perhaps double the money in a few years. He was very nice indeed and gave us several days to think about it.'

The lawyer by this time had difficulty in keeping himself quiet to listen. 'Yes. Yes, so you decided to let him have all the money to invest? Who was it? You have full details and a receipt, I suppose?'

'We have the brochure somewhere but we have not had the receipt yet but we expect it any time now,' replied Janet, looking at the clock. Oh dear, she thought, I wish I had not started this.

'Now, Mrs Willard, listen very carefully, your husband must go to the bank and stop the cheque immediately. It is very important that you do this. You are liable to lose all that money if you have not already lost it. Ask your husband to telephone me if possible, there is no time to lose.'

Janet put down the telephone. A cold feeling crept over her and she was unable to move for a short time. Then the telephone rang and jarred her out of her inertia. Answering quickly the usual enquiry about anti-freeze, she jumped up and dashed into the workshop to find Jack. 'I've been telling Mr Harrison about our investment, he said you must stop the cheque at once. How do we stop a cheque? The man has taken it away with him?'

'I will come and talk with Mr Harrison at once,' said Jack, wiping his hands as he walked. 'Have you got that folder with the name of the firm?'

'I forget where I put it but it must be around somewhere, in any case the man said we would get the receipt and details in a few days.'

Jack picked up the telephone and was connected immediately with Mr Harrison.

'Do you realize what you have done with your money?' started the lawyer at once. 'I can't impress upon you enough how important it is that you stop that cheque at once. Go into the bank immediately, take the cheque counterfoil and get the cheque stopped at once.'

'It sounds rather a drastic step to take,' started Jack, 'he was a very nice fellow and I feel sure that he was genuine, what will he think of me if I stop payment of the cheque?'

'Never mind what he thinks. Stop the cheque at once. It's your money and I only hope that it is not too late.'

'All right,' replied Jack, 'I will do so immediately.'

Janet was standing by as Jack washed his hands and prepared to go. 'Look after things here hear, I am so glad I have got you.'

Janet sat down to think. Surely that nice man would not be planning to rob us, but we have not had any kind of receipt from him or even a reply from the firm. Where did I put that paper with his phone number on? He might as well have vanished into thin air as far as I am concerned, if I have lost that card, and Janet began to worry. How awful it would be if we lost the whole of the money, and she started furiously to work to take her mind off the idea.

Jack hurried to the house to get his cheque book. There was the stub of the cheque, the last one used, made out to Tom Westlake. He put it in his pocket and drove hurriedly to the bank. He had no knowledge how banks worked but began to feel very worried now that he realized that he had handed all he had to a complete stranger. He entered the bank and asked immediately to see the manager. Jack was lucky, the manager was available and Jack was shown into his office. He produced his cheque book and explained that he had handed out a very large cheque by mistake, and wished to have it stopped. 'How do you mean stopped?' asked the manager. 'All we can do is to stop payment of the money when the recipient tries to cash the cheque. Of course, if it has already been cashed there is nothing we can do.'

'I understand that,' replied Jack.

'When do you say you gave it to the man?'

He could see that Jack held the cheque book in his hand. The bank manager took it and noticed that unfortunately Jack had omitted to fill in the name of Tom Westlake, but he remembered it as if it were written in hot coals across his chest. He had difficulty in getting his breath as the manager summoned a clerk and got him to find out the necessary information. The clerk returned to say that the cheque had not been cashed as yet. He was told to put a stop on it at once and went away to do so.

'There you are, all your worries are over. It is a very large sum, would you like to know what to do with this money? It would be wrong to leave it lying doing nothing, and actually you had the right idea, trying to invest it. There are lots of ways of using this capital to provide you with a nice little income if that is what you want, or you could leave the interest to accumulate. Shall I make an appointment for you to see our financial adviser?'

'I think I will have a talk with my wife first, after all my mother left it for us to use together. My wife is very level-headed.'

'All right,' said the manager, and shook hands. 'I hope all goes well for you.'

Janet was waiting anxiously at the garage and came forward as Jack drove up. He made a thumbs-up sign and both felt so relieved now that the worry was over. They decided to go out for a meal to celebrate.

Suddenly Janet said, 'Jack, I have been thinking. Suppose that man is on the level after all, won't he be angry when he finds out that the cheque is no good?'

'He will have to feel angry. We can easily say it is a mistake. I know that I feel a great deal happier now that I have the money still, in any case the bank manager says that we can see the financial adviser at the bank if we want to invest it. If I do go to see him I want you to come with me to hear all he has to say. He will tell us the best way to use the money and he has nothing to gain personally.'

'I am so glad,' replied Janet. 'I can't help feeling that somehow it was my fault this thing happened.'

* * *

Thursday morning arrived to find Tom still sleepless and glad to see daylight. Most of Nancy's things were packed and ready but Tom had several calls to make. First of all he had to secure accommodation for their last night in England.

Then there was a very important call to make to his bank. He had some large cheques to pay in and also to arrange for his account to be closed. He knew that it would take several days for the cheques to be cleared and for the account to be transferred. At the moment, the thought that if his plans had gone smoothly by this time Elaine would be lying dead in bed seemed to drive all other thoughts out of his head. He could not stop his mind from dwelling on his wife. The picture of her face, always kind and ready to help and willing to give so much up in order to please him during their short marriage.

I must stop this ridiculous worrying, he told himself, and forced his mind to return to the business in hand. He would take a chance and ask for some cash from the bank, no doubt someone would be happy to advise him about the transfer of his account to Hong Kong. Then he suddenly thought about his identity. He must devise some means of being able to claim his money at the other side of the world. It would still be in his old name, he remembered. Well, that would be easy. He would keep his credit card hidden away somewhere. Fortunately he had not yet destroyed it.

He entered the bank. The first clerk recognized him and took the paying-in book containing a great deal of money in one form or another from him. Tom felt constrained to give some kind of explanation and said that he had suddenly to go abroad and would be away some time. He had realized some capital and wished to pay it in and to transfer his account when complete to a bank in Hong Kong. Perhaps he could have some advice as to which bank it should be?

'We will see to that for you,' said the clerk. 'Can you call back in a few days?'

'No, that's just the trouble. I have to catch a plane tomorrow. That's why I have called in now. First of all I have to cash a cheque for rather a large amount to use on my journey.'

'How much do you wish to draw?' asked the clerk.

'Well, seeing that I have just paid in a very large amount, I wish to draw several hundred pounds to take with me, I have my air ticket to pay for and several bills to settle, shall we say £15,000?'

'Just a minute sir, I will see how your credit stands. As you know we can advance cash if required but I am not sure that you can overdraw until some of those cheques you are paying in are cleared.'

Tom felt annoyed but not very surprised to hear this, he didn't want to cause too much fuss so settled for what the clerk suggested. He knew that he dared not draw too much attention to himself and left the bank feeling disappointed. He had less than he had asked for but a sense of relief that no leading questions had been asked. There were other things to think of at the moment. He had to sell the car and had thought out a scheme during the night. He would negotiate a sale of the car to a garage on condition that he could drive it to the airport. He had at first thought to stay overnight at a hotel near to the hotel, but realized that it was risky. That would be the first place anyone would look for him if trying to trace his movements. After all, he was not really sure that Elaine was dead.

Tom's next call was to collect the tickets at the airport and as he parked the car at Heathrow he could not help taking a look around. Then, straightening himself up, he realized that he had started to look furtive and that was the first thing that might draw attention to him. He found that the tickets were handed over without any fuss. Now he could go back to Nancy's flat and get things ready for leaving everything behind for good.

It was breakfast time in Nancy's flat. Nancy had taken his advice and had told no one that she was leaving. If their plans went well there would be no way at all for anyone to trace her. A hurried breakfast was taken, the remainder of the clothes packed and the couple left the flat unobserved and retaining the key. As they left the flat each assumed a new name and a new passport came to hand ready for use.

Tom secretly thought with dread of the long journey in Nancy's company and tried to console himself that he would feel better when the strain of the long journey was over. He had negotiated the sale of the car and had arranged to hand it over at the airport to the buyer's representative. He was not very pleased with the price offered but had to agree. He had to call once more at the bank. It seemed that it had taken some time for a Hong Kong bank to be found that would agree to the transaction and Tom still had to sit for a time biting his nails and trying not to look at everyone as they entered the door of the bank. Each hour that he maintained his own appearance was adding more and more to the risk of someone he knew seeing him and accosting him. Eventually to his great relief he was told that a bank had been found and that his current account would be transferred as soon as it was up to date and practicable.

* * *

On Thursday afternoon Elaine thought that she could safely come home without encountering Tom, she felt that she could not possibly speak to him again until this ridiculous idea of robbing people and leaving the country with the proceeds had grown stale and he had forgotten it. It must be some hideous joke, she felt sure, and he would soon come to his senses.

She took her shopping into the kitchen to unload, tea, sugar, lots of odds and ends and right at the bottom of the basket a fresh jar of malted milk. She lifted the old jar from the shelf, replaced it with the new and threw the near-empty one into the trash can without a thought. Making a cup of tea she sat down to look at a woman's magazine she had bought.

Three cups of tea and an hour later she began to wonder if she would ever see Tom again. I was a fool to refuse to go along with him, perhaps I could have managed to discourage him. Finally she could keep from wondering no longer and realized that she could telephone his office and find out more.

She looked at the clock and realized that she must telephone the office soon or it would be closed. She picked the telephone up, her hand trembling. A strange voice answered.

'Yes, this is Mrs Westlake, could I speak to my husband please?'

The answer came 'Mr Westlake is not here, he has not been to the office for two days. His secretary is away as well, she has taken a few days off as she is not well.'

'Do you expect Mr Westlake to call back to the office today?'

'I don't really know, if you will wait a few moments I will try to find out.' The phone was put down and after a short time a voice said, 'Who is that please?'

'I am Mrs Westlake, I am enquiring if my husband is expected back at the office today.'

'I am very sorry Mrs Westlake, I have no idea where your husband is, he has strict instructions always to let someone at the office know where he can be contacted. He has not done this and I am afraid he will have to provide a very good explanation as to his movements or he will find himself without a job. I am very sorry Mrs Westlake but I am quite angry at your husband's behaviour. It is not like him. He is a well-trained and useful negotiator and has just the right personality for his job, but he seems to have completely changed and goodness knows where he has got to.'

Elaine began to feel angry and said, 'Has it not occurred to you that something may have happened to him?'

The manager seemed rather surprised at her suggestion and after a pause said, 'Sorry Mrs Westlake, there is nothing more I can add. Goodbye.'

Elaine began to realize that she might never see Tom again. I will have to get something to do, she told herself, and thought that it was a good thing that she did not have a young child to look after. It was Tom who kept saying that we must get a home of our own before starting a family. Now he has a home, with someone else and with stolen money. She finally broke down in tears. I have to meet this alone and pretend that all is well. I can't tell Daddy, he never liked Tom anyway, and would probably say 'I told you so'. I must cheer myself up and look happy, and if asked I will say that Tom has had to go away on business.

* * *

Tom and Nancy were ready to start for the airport. The driver who was taking Tom's car to the airport to bring it back to the new owner was expected. Nancy seemed to have a lot of small and fussy luggage.

'What have you got in all that?' asked Tom.

'Oh, just little things I can't do without.'

'Show me your handbag,' said Tom, and Nancy handed it over looking surprised. Tom opened it and tipped everything out. The first thing he picked up after removing the small, well-filled purse was a credit card. 'There you are. What's this?' asked Tom angrily. 'I told you to destroy everything you had in your old name. Your name is now Westland. You agreed to this partnership, now you are going to let me down through sheer carelessness. It's not too late to back out now if you are not sure about it.'

Delving deeper he found a packet of letters with envelopes, complete with address intact. He found a credit card also in her own name. Looking at Nancy, he realized that she really was little better than a child in experience.

'Have you never been on a plane before?' he asked.

He remembered the old saying about a woman scorned, and realized that he must not make an enemy of Nancy. He asked again and Nancy replied, 'You said that I would never return,

I have always longed to go in an aeroplane, so I had to take everything I value.'

'You can come back to England later on if you don't like it, you know. You are now Mrs Westland, so any letters you carry should be addressed to that name. Better still, get rid of the letters. Come along, let me see what else you have got packed. I don't want anyone, not anyone, to know where we have gone. I have taken money that belongs to the firm, if I am found I could be sent to jail for a long time and perhaps you could too, so you must see how careful we must be.'

He told her to go down and sit in the lounge and wait for him, meanwhile he hurriedly sorted through the rest of her cases and picked out any incriminating matter to destroy.

The car driver from the garage arrived in good time and helped to carry the luggage out to the car. It was heavily loaded when all was stowed away and they set off for the airport. Tom reflected that Nancy was going to be difficult to cope with. How much better it would have been if Elaine had agreed to come with me he thought. She was so sensible and helpful.

'Do you feel all right?' asked the garage man who was sitting behind Tom. 'You seem to be taking unnecessary risks.'

'I am sorry,' said Tom. 'My mind was on other things.'

The thought that he was leaving everything behind that he knew and had loved seemed to occupy his mind, and he suddenly realized that he was overtaking at great speed and a car was pulling out into his path. It was quite impossible to avoid it and the car went out of control and right into the path of a huge and fully loaded pantechnicon. Not one of the three occupants of the car knew what was happening. They were all three trapped and crushed hopelessly.

19

It was Saturday and Jack and Janet had put in some hard work at the garage and felt that the week had seemed a long one. There was a great deal to do; many of their regular customers called for petrol on Saturday and there were always casual people who called as they passed on their way to the country or to fill up for a Sunday trip. Sometimes a customer who had arranged to hire a car had to be attended to on Sunday. Insurance cover had to be arranged and there was always fuel to be supplied. Janet wanted to go home and said to Jack, 'I don't know why I feel so tired lately. I sleep well yet I never feel hungry and always seem tired.'

'I am not very surprised,' said Jack. 'After all, a great deal has happened to us lately but do you think that you should see a doctor?'

He had noticed that Janet looked tired lately, she worked very hard at the cottage and kept it spotless, also she was determined to keep the rose garden looking as good as it did when Jack's mother was there. Of course she had had the old gardener one day a week. What a pity he can't come now. He must be old and he is very lame, poor chap, Jack thought.

At last Jack said, 'I think I have finished for the day, for the week actually. Is there a c? booked out for tomorrow? I thought I saw that young man come into the office. You know, the one who has had it for several Sundays.'

'Yes, he did call but it was only to ask if he could book one for next week. He has to go to see about a new job. I have booked it for him and he has paid a deposit.'

Soon they were on their way home. After tea they settled down to look at television and the first picture that came on to the screen was during the news. There had been a triple car crash, just outside Heathrow. Looking at the picture of the wrecked cars a number plate stood out clearly. Suddenly Janet exclaimed, 'Look at that number plate! I have seen it before, now where? I know I have seen it. It struck me as being so funny. It was C and a number, J.A.W. my initials, Janet Agnes Willard. Oh, I have it, it was the fellow we gave our cheque to. It was his car. I saw it standing outside our window when he was coming in to see us about our investments.'

'Really, are you sure?'

'Yes, that was the car.'

'It was probably hired anyway,' said Jack. 'Perhaps we shall hear more about it. The news said that three people were killed didn't it?'

'Yes. Oh dear, I feel quite faint.'

'Don't be silly dear, we have got the money back and there is nothing to worry about. I wonder what the doctor will say on Monday? Suppose we have a happy event to look forward to. Do you think it could be possible?'

'We shall see on Monday,' said Janet, looking shy and blushing engagingly.